Ella and the Timeless

Andrew S. French

Neonoir Books

Also by Andrew S. French

The Arcane Supernatural Thriller Series

The Arcane

The Arcane Identity

The Arcane Quest

The Arcane Ultimatum

The Ella Finn Fantasy Series

Ella and the Elementals

Ella and the Multiverse

Ella and the Monsters

Ella and the Dreamers

Supernatural Short Stories

Dead Souls

Dead Souls II

Dead Souls III

The Shadow

Science Fiction

The Time Traveller's Murder

The Mercy Sleep

Bodies

Another Girl, Another Planet

The Thief of Time Trilogy

The Queens of Heaven

The Queens of Time

The Queens of Space

Writing as A. S. French

Crime Fiction and Thrillers

The Astrid Snow series

Don't Fear the Reaper

The Killing Moon

Lost in America

Gone to Texas

The Final Girl

Snowstorm: An Astrid Snow Collection

Astrid Snow: The Collection

The Detective Jen Flowers series

The Hashtag Killer

Serial Killer

Night Killer

The Killer Inside Them

Inspector Flowers Collection: Books 1-4

Northern Crime Fiction

Where The Bodies Are Buried

Bodies of Evidence

The Lulu Chase Mysteries

The Strange Case of Madam X

Chapter 1

Awake

The world around her was dead.

Ella opened her eyes, her head swimming with a dull throb. Every breath she took felt like she was inhaling dirt. She blinked a few times, her vision struggling to adjust to the muted light. The surface beneath her was hard and cracked, rough against her skin. She touched cold grit under her fingers. Concrete?

She forced herself to sit up, her body protesting each movement. Her muscles ached, and her clothes were soaked, still clinging to her from...what? Her brain was sluggish, struggling to recall how she got there. The last thing she remembered was sinking into the water. Lyssa. The relics. Her friends. Her parents.

But now? Everything felt wrong.

Ella ran a hand through her damp hair, pushing it away from her face. The air stank of smoke and something metallic, like rust. She squinted against the overcast sky, a dull, hazy grey stretching above her, blocking the sun. No warmth, no birds. Just silence.

A sense of unease slithered up her spine. The landscape

was alien in its desolation. She was sitting in the middle of a broken road, the pavement jagged and torn apart, as if some immense force had ripped it open. Weeds grew out of the cracks, dry and brittle. Rusted husks of cars lay scattered around like forgotten toys, windows smashed in, metal twisted and eroded by time. There was no movement. No sound, save for the distant, steady hum she couldn't identify.

She stood, wobbling as her legs trembled. Her limbs were stiff, her skin cold. She rubbed her arms, trying to bring warmth back into her body. Her stomach tightened with a growing sense of dread. She didn't recognise the place. She recognised nothing.

Where the hell was she?

'Mum?' Her voice cracked, weak and hoarse. 'Dad?'

No answer. The silence was deafening. Panic gripped her chest, squeezing tighter with every second. She took a few tentative steps forward, her boots scraping against the broken road. The world felt empty and abandoned. No sign of life. Her heart raced as she studied her surroundings. Was this a nightmare? Had she died? Was this what the afterlife looked like?

'Seraphina?' Ella tried again, louder this time. 'Peg? Kitty? Anyone?'

Nothing. Not even an echo.

A tremor passed through her, cold and sudden. She wrapped her arms around herself, feeling exposed in the empty wasteland. She started walking, her steps slow and deliberate, trying to understand what had happened. Everything was a blur. One moment she was sinking, the next, this.

As she rounded the corner of an abandoned building, the sheer scope of the devastation hit her. The city—if you could even call it that—was in ruins. Towers that once reached for the sky were reduced to skeletal frames, their windows shattered, and their walls crumbling. Bridges lay in pieces, roads twisted and broken. The remnants of human life were everywhere—overturned trucks, decaying storefronts, scattered debris—but no people.

It was like the world had ended.

She stopped beside an old, faded billboard. The edges were peeling, and graffiti covered the bottom half, but the date at the top was still clear: January 2075.

'What...?' Ella blinked, stepping closer. Her pulse quickened. That couldn't be right. She swallowed, her throat dry. 'That's not possible...'

Her hand hovered over the billboard, her fingers trembling. It had been 2025 when she went into the water. She stared at the date again, disbelief washing over her. Fifty years? Could she have been unconscious for that long?

Wouldn't she be dead? Grown-up?

A nauseating pit formed in her stomach as she stumbled backwards, the weight of the realisation crashing down on her. No, it couldn't be. She couldn't have been out for fifty years. There had to be a mistake. Some trick. Maybe this was all a hallucination.

But the air was too cold, the ground too solid beneath her feet. The ache in her muscles and the hunger gnawing at her stomach were all too real. Her brain throbbed with a thousand questions as she tried to wrap her head around it. Fifty years. Her parents. Her friends. Everyone she knew— were they even alive? Could they have survived this? Whatever this was?

A sudden noise jerked her from her thoughts. A low, metallic hum echoed from the distance, growing louder and vibrating. She crouched behind a rusted-out car, her heart hammering in her chest.

What was that?

The vibration grew into a whirring sound, and then she saw them. Drones. Sleek, spherical machines with glowing red eyes scanned everywhere. They hovered above the ruins, moving with unnerving precision, their dark metallic bodies glinting in the gloom. She held her breath, ducking lower behind the car. She had no idea what the machines were, but they made her skin crawl. They moved in synchronised patterns, sweeping the area as if searching for something. Or someone.

Her muscles tensed. The hair on the back of her neck stood up. Whatever those drones were, they weren't human-made, unlike anything she'd ever seen. Ella edged around the car, keeping low, her breath shallow as she watched the machines. Her heart threatened to burst, pounding so hard she was sure they'd hear it. She needed to get away.

She darted across the street, ducking into the shadow of a half-collapsed building. Her body screamed in protest, the sudden movement sending sharp agony through her bones, but she pushed through it. There was no time to think about the pain.

The drones soared overhead. She flattened herself against the wall, holding her breath. Sweat slicked her palms as she waited, focused on the hovering machines. She didn't know what would happen if they spotted her and didn't want to find out.

After an eternity, the drones moved on, disappearing into the distance. Ella exhaled, slumping against the wall, her legs shaking.

She couldn't stay there - wherever *there* was.

Her gaze drifted back to the twisted remnants of the

city. She grew up in London, leaving at twelve when her mum and dad disappeared and going to live with her horrible cousins in Redcar. Her parents eventually returned, and they all stayed in the northeast, but she didn't recognise the broken city. Was she even in England? The billboard was in English, so she assumed so.

She remembered being on the island as it sank, seeing her parents and friends struggling as she did, and that had been in the North Sea, close to Britain. So she'd travelled through time and space.

But how? And where were the others? Were they like her, lost in the broken city? She gazed into the ruins. It was hard to tell how much time had passed, but everything looked old. Abandoned. How long had those alien things been there? And where was everyone?

Ella pushed away from the wall and moved again, keeping to the shadows. Her mind whirled with questions, but there were no answers. Not yet.

She wandered through the streets, stepping over rubble and debris, her thoughts chaotic. The buildings loomed over her, hollow and empty, their windows dark and lifeless. No people. No animals. Not even the wind seemed to stir the air.

It was as if silence had swallowed the world.

Her stomach twisted with hunger, but there was no food in sight. She tried not to think about it, focusing instead on finding some clue. Something that could tell her what had happened. Where had the invaders come from? How had she survived in the sea when the island sank?

And how to get back.

A flicker of movement caught her eye. She froze, ducking behind a wall, her breath frozen. A figure moved in the shadows across the street. A man—ragged, filthy, and hunched over as if in pain. His clothes were torn, his face gaunt and hollow.

She hesitated for a moment, then stepped out of her hiding place. 'Hey,' she called.

His head snapped up, eyes wide with fear. He backed away with his lips trembling.

'Wait!' Ella held up her hands to show she wasn't a threat. 'I won't hurt you.'

But he didn't listen. He scrambled backwards, his feet slipping on the rubble before he turned and bolted down the alley, disappearing into the shadows. She stood stunned, her chest throbbing. What had scared him so much? Was it her? Or something else?

She glanced around, feeling the tension in the air thickening. The hum from earlier was back, louder now, pulsing through the ground. Her skin prickled, and a cold sweat broke out across her forehead.

Something was coming.

Ella didn't wait to find out what. She turned and ran, her boots slapping against the cracked pavement as she darted through the ruins. The distant footsteps echoed behind her—heavy, deliberate, inhuman. Her lungs burned, her muscles screaming in protest, but she didn't stop.

As she reached the ruin's edge, she saw a massive alien structure towering over the landscape. Dark, twisted, and pulsing with light. It stretched into the sky. It was unlike anything Ella had ever seen, yet something about it felt familiar.

She moved toward it, her breath coming in ragged gasps. The world around her was too quiet, too still. But she couldn't shake the feeling that an unseen presence observed her. She dug her fingers into her palms and tried not to worry about her missing parents and friends.

But it was impossible.

Then something hit her.

The impact sent Ella sprawling, her chin scraping against broken concrete. Stars burst behind her eyes as a weight pressed down on her back, pinning her to the ground. The metallic taste of blood filled her mouth.

'Don't move,' a voice whispered. 'They're right above us.'

The pressure on her spine lessened, but Ella stayed frozen, her heart thundering against the cold ground. She tasted dirt and copper, feeling warm blood trickle down her chin. The hum of drones grew louder, their scanners painting the ruins in crimson light.

'Breathe slower,' the voice commanded. 'They track heat signatures.'

Ella forced herself to take shallow breaths, fighting against her instinct to gulp air. The person above her shifted, and she glimpsed worn combat boots.

The drones passed overhead, their whirring growing fainter until silence settled again. Only then did the weight lift.

'Sorry about that.' The voice belonged to a girl not much older than Ella. She offered a calloused hand. 'Had to tackle you. You were running straight into a patrol zone.'

Ella accepted the help, wincing as she stood. The girl was tall and wiry, with close-cropped black hair and dark skin weathered by exposure. A network of pale scars crossed her bare arms, telling stories Ella wasn't sure she wanted to hear.

'I'm Amari,' she said, checking their surroundings. She moved like a predator, all controlled energy and watchful eyes. 'And you're brave or stupid to be out here alone.'

Ella touched her bleeding chin. 'I didn't plan this.'

'Nobody plans anything anymore.' Amari's laugh was hollow. She pulled a dirty cloth from her pocket and handed it to Ella. 'Here. You're leaving a blood trail.'

'Thanks.' Ella pressed the material to her skin, studying Amari's face. The girl couldn't have been more than sixteen, but her eyes were ancient. 'I'm Ella. And I'm lost.'

Amari's eyebrows rose. 'Lost? In a restricted zone?' She crossed her arms. 'Where's your sector badge? Your ration card?'

Ella's stomach twisted. 'I don't have those things. I just woke up here.' The words sounded ridiculous even to her ears. 'I know this will sound crazy, but I think I've travelled through time. It was 2025 when I...' She trailed off, seeing Amari's expression harden.

'If you're a Runner, say so,' Amari said. 'I don't care. But don't feed me temporal displacement bullshit. The Invaders use that line to catch sympathisers.'

'The Invaders?'

Amari's hand went to something strapped to her thigh – a weapon, Ella realised with a jolt. 'Okay, now I know you're playing me. Everyone knows who the Invaders are.' Her voice dropped to a dangerous whisper. 'Did they send you? Are you one of their puppets?'

'No! I swear, I'm not...' Ella's lips trembled. The exhaustion, hunger, and fear crashed over her in a wave. 'The last thing I remember was being in the North Sea. The island was sinking, and my parents...' Her throat closed up. 'God, my mum and dad. They were right there with me, and now...'

Something in her tone must have convinced Amari because the older girl's stance softened. She glanced at the alien structure looming in the distance, then back at Ella.

'You know nothing, do you?' Amari sighed, running a

hand through her short hair. 'That thing you're staring at? That's a Harvest Tower. The Invaders built them after they arrived. They're...' She swallowed hard. 'That's where they process humans.'

Ella shivered. 'What do you mean, process?'

'They drain us,' Amari said. 'Our life force, our essence, whatever you want to call it. They hook people up to these machines and...' She looked away. 'They keep you alive as long as possible, feeding off your energy until there's nothing left but a husk.'

Ella's knees weakened. She stumbled back until she hit a wall, sliding down to sit on the ground. 'No. No, that can't be...'

'Hey.' Amari crouched beside her, voice gentler now. 'Look, I don't understand how you got here or what's happening, but you can't stay out in the open. The next patrol might not be just drones.'

'What could be worse than drones?'

Amari's face darkened. 'Harvesters. They're like...' She gestured vaguely. 'Imagine if a spider and a machine had a baby, then gave it a taste for human fear. That's a Harvester.'

A distant screech echoed through the ruins, making both girls flinch. Amari stood, offering her hand again.

'Come on. I know somewhere safe. Well, safer than here.' She pulled Ella up. 'My group has a hideout nearby. We can get you food, clean that cut, and figure out what's happening.'

Ella hesitated. 'Your group?'

'The Resistance.' Amari's smile was fierce and proud. 'What's left of it, anyway. We're not much, but we're still fighting.' She rechecked her surroundings, ever vigilant. 'So what do you say? Trust a stranger in this nightmare, or take your chances with the Invaders?'

Another screech, closer this time. Ella shuddered. 'Lead the way.'

They moved through the ruins like ghosts, Amari teaching Ella to step silently and where to place her feet to avoid loose debris. They froze at every sound, and each shadow could hide death. The constant tension made Ella's muscles ache more.

'Almost there,' Amari whispered after what felt like hours. 'Just have to get through the Dead Zone.'

'The Dead Zone?'

'See how nothing grows here? Not even weeds?' Amari pointed to the barren ground. 'The Invaders' technology poisons the earth. Creates these dead patches where nothing can survive.' She spat. 'They're killing the entire planet, bit by bit.'

Ella thought of the Book of All Life, of its connection to Elementals and their realm. If she still had it, maybe... But it was lost in the sea with everything she'd known.

A low rumble shook the ground. Amari grabbed Ella's arm, yanking her behind a fallen column.

'Don't. Move.' Amari's whispered against Ella's ear. 'Harvester.'

The thing that emerged from the shadows made Ella's blood freeze. Amari's description hadn't done it justice. It moved on multiple jointed legs, its body a twisted mass of metal and organic matter. Where its face should have been, dozens of red sensors pulsed in rhythmic patterns. It dragged something behind it – a net filled with dark shapes that Ella refused to look at too closely.

She pressed her hand against her mouth, fighting the urge to scream. Beside her, Amari was still as stone, breathing so shallow she might not have been breathing at all.

The Harvester paused, its sensors sweeping the area. Ella's heart pounded so hard she was sure the thing would hear it. Seconds stretched into eternities.

Then, it moved on, disappearing into the ruins with its terrible cargo. Only then did Amari release her grip on Ella.

'Now you know,' Amari said. 'That's what we're fighting against. That's what they've turned our world into.' She stared at Ella. 'Still want to come with me?'

Ella looked at the Harvest Tower in the distance and then at Amari. She thought of her parents, her friends, everyone she'd lost. Were they somewhere in this nightmare future? Or had they...

No. She couldn't think about that now.

'Yes,' Ella said, surprised by the strength in her voice. 'Show me everything.'

Chapter 2

The New World

Ella crouched in the shadows of a crumbling wall, the scent of damp and decay clinging to the air around her. She wiped her palms on her torn trousers, the rough fabric scraping her skin. The cold bit into her bones, but it wasn't the kind of cold she was used to. This wasn't the chill of a late autumn night in England—it was deeper, a cold that had settled into the earth after years of neglect.

Ahead, the street was quiet, a graveyard of the life that once bustled everywhere. There was no sound except for the occasional distant hum of patrolling alien machines, predators stalking their prey. She sensed the weight of it in the air—the oppressive presence of something inhuman.

Her stomach tightened as she peered down at the street, seeing the shattered windows of the buildings, the faded shop signs hanging broken, the vehicles abandoned and rusting. Everything was in ruins, like the world had stopped caring long ago.

She followed behind Amari, no words between them.

Her boots crunched over gravel and glass as she navi-

12

gated the urban landscape. The sound was too loud, almost invasive in the oppressive quiet. She skirted around massive piles of debris and collapsed buildings. Burnt-out cars sat strewn across the streets; some flipped over like toys. She stumbled through a ghost town, a forgotten relic from a world that no longer existed.

Then, she noticed something: symbols painted on walls, crude and uneven. She didn't understand some words, but others were clear—warnings and messages scratched into the stone.

Stay low. Don't trust them.

Run if you see the eyes.

Ella's stomach twisted. Her breath fogged in front of her face, and for a moment, she wondered how long it had been since she'd seen a sunrise. The sky was overcast as if the sun had given up on the place. She squinted at the grey haze, despair creeping in.

'Fifty years,' she muttered, shaking her head. 'More like fifty lifetimes.'

Her throat felt dry, the words catching as she spoke them, as if giving voice to the thought made it real. She was in the future—too far ahead for anything she knew to matter. Her family, her friends, everything she'd fought for was gone, buried beneath the wreckage of this terrible world.

A noise snapped her attention back to the street, and she tensed, pressing against the wall. Like a swarm of bees, a low hum vibrated in the distance. Ella gripped the edge of the stone, knuckles turning white as she peered around the corner.

'Quiet,' Amari hissed, pointing forward.

It was one of them.

A drone. Alien tech. It hovered above the ground, sleek

and menacing, its black surface gleaming in the gloom. It was like nothing she'd ever seen—no wires, no rotors, just a seamless machine that defied gravity, floating with an eerie grace. The red eye in its centre glowed, sweeping back and forth, scanning for prey.

Ella's chest throbbed, and she flattened her spine against the wall, holding her breath. She didn't dare move. The machine hovered closer, the hum intensifying as it neared. She felt the vibration in her teeth, a low vibrating sound that made her want to scream and run. But she stayed still, her body rigid, every muscle tensed. The drone passed by, only inches from their hiding spot, the red eye flickering as it scanned the area. She gasped for air, her heart hammering against her ribs.

Then, just as quickly as it had appeared, the drone drifted away, disappearing into the foggy distance. She exhaled, her legs trembling as the tension released from her. She sank to the ground, pressing her spine against the stone, her eyes closing.

What is this place?

'Are you okay?' Amari said.

Ella opened her eyes. 'I'm fine.'

She stared at the wreckage around her, trying to understand it. This wasn't the England she knew. It was something else, something broken, something alien—the symbols painted on the walls—warnings, desperate cries for help—made sense now. Whoever had been before her had known the dangers and had tried to warn others, but it hadn't been enough. The city was empty and desolate, save for the drones and whatever lurked in the shadows.

Except for her and Amari.

Ella studied the teenage girl, wondering if she should trust her. She could be anybody, leading her into a trap.

Maybe she was an alien in disguise. Was she Lyssa? Had The Soulless followed her there? Perhaps it was all an illusion created by Lyssa. But why?

She stood, her muscles protesting.

Move. Don't stand still. Standing still will get you killed.

The thought came unbidden, instinctual. It had been her practice, even before all of this. Always moving, always looking for a way forward.

'We have to keep moving,' Amari said.

Ella nodded. 'Where are we going?'

'To safety,' the other girl replied.

Ella pulled her jacket tighter around her shoulders and moved, keeping low, her eyes darting from shadow to shadow. The streets grew narrower as they strode deeper into the city, the buildings looming overhead like silent sentinels.

The entrance to the Resistance hideout wasn't what Ella expected. Amari led her through a maze of ruined structures to an old Underground station, its sign long since fallen away. Rust-coloured stains marked the surface, and Ella tried not to think about what might have caused them.

'Watch your step,' Amari whispered, pulling aside a sheet of corroded metal to reveal a narrow corridor. 'And whatever you do, don't touch the walls in this next part.'

'Why not?'

Amari's face was grim. 'Because they're coated with sensor gel. One touch sets off the defence systems.' She demonstrated how to move, pressing close to the centre of the passage. 'The Invaders can't detect it, but it knows human DNA. It keeps us safe and them out.'

Ella followed Amari, her shoulders aching as they navigated the tight space. The passage seemed to go on forever, twisting downward in a gentle spiral. The air grew colder, damper. Their footsteps echoed despite their care, the sound bouncing off unseen walls. Her eyes adjusted to the gloom, her boots scratching against the stone. It was a small area, cramped and filled with people—men, women, children—all huddled together in makeshift tents and corners. Their faces were hollow, gaunt from hiding and scraping by. Heat came from several fires, their light casting flickering shadows everywhere.

Conversations were hushed, whispers carried on the air like secrets not meant to be heard. Ella crept through the space, scanning the faces around her. No one seemed to notice her at first, too absorbed in their world of survival.

'How do you even find places like this?' Ella asked, trying to distract herself from the growing claustrophobia.

'We don't find them.' Amari's voice was soft, almost reverent. 'The old resistance built them.' She paused at a junction, touching a series of notches in the floor. 'My parents helped design this network. Dad was an engineer, and Mum was a geologist. They knew the city's guts better than anyone.'

The way Amari said 'was' made Ella's heart ache. 'What happened to them?'

'Same thing that happened to everyone else who fought back.' Amari's voice was flat. 'They got processed.' She moved forward again, faster now. 'Come on. We're almost there.'

They emerged into a larger space, and Ella gasped. The old Underground platform had been transformed into something out of a sci-fi film. Strings of lights crisscrossed the ceiling, casting a warm glow over makeshift living quarters. People moved about with purpose – some tending to hydroponic gardens that climbed the walls, others hunched over workbenches filled with salvaged technology.

'Welcome to Haven Station,' Amari said, a hint of pride breaking through her hardened exterior. 'One of the last free human settlements in London.'

So, she was in London – a future version of the city where she grew up.

A boy about Amari's age approached them, his dark eyes narrowing at the sight of Ella. He moved with a slight limp, and the left side of his face bore a lattice of silvery scars that disappeared beneath his collar.

'Picked up another stray, Amari?' His accent was Northern, Manchester, maybe. 'Or is this one different?'

'She's different, Ash.' Amari touched his arm– a casual yet intimate gesture that Ella felt like she was intruding. 'Found her in Sector Seven, running blind into a patrol zone. Says she's from 2025.'

Ash's eyebrows shot up. 'That's new.' He studied Ella. 'You sure she's not—'

'I'm sure.' Amari cut him off. 'You didn't see her face when we encountered the Harvester. No puppet could fake that kind of fear.' She turned to Ella. 'Ash is our tech expert. If anyone can figure out how you got here, it's him.'

Ella shifted under Ash's scrutiny. 'I don't understand it myself. I was in the North Sea one minute, and the next...'

'The North Sea?' A new voice joined the conversation. An older woman emerged from the shadows, her silver hair pulled back in a severe braid. She moved with quiet authority, and everyone around them seemed to straighten up. 'Did you say the North Sea?'

Amari stepped forward. 'Commander Chen, I can explain—'

The woman held up a hand, silencing Amari. Her eyes never left Ella's face. 'What year did you say you came from?'

'2025,' Ella answered. Something about the woman's intense gaze made her want to step back. 'I was on an island with my parents and friends. It was sinking, and there were these relics—'

'The Elemental Purge.' Commander Chen said.

The temperature in the room dropped. Amari and Ash exchanged glances.

'Commander?' Ash ventured. 'What's going on?'

Chen straightened, her expression hardening. 'Amari, get her cleaned up and fed. Then bring her to my quarters.' She turned to leave, then paused. 'And Amari? Don't let her out of your sight.'

They watched Chen disappear into the shadows.

Amari sighed. 'Well, that was interesting.'

'What was that about?' Ella asked. 'The Elemental Purge – how does she know about them?'

'Later.' Amari took her arm, steering her toward a makeshift medical bay. 'First, let's get that cut looked at. And maybe find you some clobber that doesn't scream '2025 fashion disaster."

An hour later, Ella sat on a worn sofa in what passed for a common area, wearing salvaged clothes Amari had scrounged up – heavy boots, reinforced trousers, and a dark jacket lined with some protective material she didn't recognise. They'd treated her chin with a strange gel that numbed the pain and accelerated healing. The food they'd given her was bland but filling – some synthetic protein and vegetables from the hydroponic gardens.

Ash sat across from her, tinkering with a device resembling a cross between a smartphone and a medical scanner. He had said little, but his eyes darted to her when he thought she wasn't looking.

'Just ask,' Ella suggested. 'Whatever you want to know.'

He set down his tools. 'It's not that simple. Time travel – real time travel – it's impossible. The Invaders have tried it. We know they have. But the energy requirements alone...' He shook his head. 'But there are rumours they have something which can see into the future. And yet you appear, wearing clothes that haven't been manufactured in sixty years, with cellular degradation patterns that make no sense.'

'What do you mean?'

'Your cells.' He held up the scanner. 'They show no signs of ageing between 2025 and now. It's like you just... skipped everything in between. That's not possible. Unless...'

'Unless what?'

An explosion rocked the station before he could answer. Alarms blared, and the warm lights shifted to pulsing red. Amari appeared from nowhere, weapon drawn.

'We've got trouble,' she said. 'Big trouble. They found an entrance.'

Ash grabbed equipment from nearby tables. 'Which one?'

'Northern tunnel. The sensor gel's been compromised.' Amari's voice was tight with tension. 'They're sending in Crawlers.'

'What are Crawlers?' Ella asked though she wasn't sure she wanted to know.

'Think of them as baby Harvesters,' Ash said. 'Smaller, faster, harder to kill.' He tossed Amari what looked like a modified grenade. 'How many?'

'At least a dozen. Maybe more.' Amari caught the grenade one-handed. 'Commander Chen's ordering an evacuation to the lower levels.'

Another explosion, closer this time. The sound of gunfire echoed through the tunnels, followed by screams.

'Too late,' Amari said. 'They're inside.'

The first Crawler appeared at the far end of the platform – a writhing mass of metal and synthetic muscle, no bigger than a large dog. Its segmented body rippled as it moved, sensors pulsing with an eager red light. Behind it, more shapes emerged from the darkness.

'Ella, run,' Amari said. 'Go with the others. Ash will show you the way.'

'What about you?'

Amari's smile was fierce. 'Someone has to hold them off.' She squared her shoulders, weapon raised. 'Go. Now!'

Ash grabbed Ella's arm, pulling her toward a maintenance tunnel. Behind them, Amari's weapon fired with a sound like thunder. The Crawlers screeched, their cries mixing with the ongoing alarms into a hellish cacophony.

'She'll be okay,' Ash said, though Ella wasn't sure if he was trying to convince her or himself. 'Amari knows what she's doing.'

They ran through maintenance tunnels that seemed to go on forever, joining a stream of other refugees heading deeper underground. Children cried, adults shouted instructions, and the constant sound of pursuit was beneath it all.

'In here!' Commander Chen appeared, ushering people into a hidden chamber.

Ella followed Ash inside. It was large but crowded, filled with anxious faces and hastily grabbed supplies. Commander Chen sealed the heavy door behind them, engaging a series of locks that hissed with hydraulic pressure.

'Will that hold them?' someone asked.

'Long enough.' The Commander's voice was grim. She turned to Ella. 'This is why we needed to talk. They're not just looking for survivors. They're searching for you.'

'Me? But why?'

'Because,' Commander Chen said, 'you travelled through time.'

A bang on the door made everyone jump. Then another. And another.

'They're here,' Ash whispered.

Chen drew a weapon Ella didn't recognise – something that hummed with energy. 'Ash, take her through the emergency tunnel. Get her to the East Haven. Find Doctor Santos – he'll know what to do.'

'What about you?' Ash wondered, though he was already moving toward a concealed panel in the wall.

'We'll hold them here.' The Commander's voice was steel. 'Now go. And Ella?' Their eyes met. 'Whatever you do, don't let them take you alive. What they'd learn from you...' She turned away. 'It would be the end of everything.'

The panel slid open, revealing a narrow tunnel lit by strips of pale blue light. Ash pulled Ella inside just as the banging on the entrance reached a crescendo.

The last thing Ella saw before the panel closed was Commander Chen, standing tall amid her people, weapon raised as the door buckled.

'Come on,' Ash said, his voice thick. 'We need to move.'

They crawled through the tunnel, the sounds of battle growing fainter behind them. Ella's mind was a storm of questions, but she forced herself to focus on moving forward. One hand in front of the other. Don't think about Amari. Don't think about the Commander. Don't think about anything except survival.

After what felt like hours, the tunnel widened into a

small chamber with multiple exits. Ash paused, consulting a holographic map projected from a device on his wrist.

'East tunnel,' he muttered. 'Should take us right to—'

He froze. Ella heard it, too – a skittering sound coming from one of the other tunnels. Then another, from a different direction.

'They're in the maintenance network,' Ash whispered. His face was pale in the blue light. 'They're herding us.'

'What do we do?'

He grabbed her hand, pulling her toward the east tunnel. 'We run. And we pray.'

They sprinted through the darkness, the sound of pursuit growing closer with each step. Ella's lungs burned, her legs trembled, but she kept moving. The tunnel seemed endless, each turn revealing only more darkness.

'Almost there,' Ash panted. 'Just a little—'

Something burst from a side tunnel, slamming into him. Ash cried out as he hit the wall, the Crawler's metallic limbs wrapping around him like a grotesque embrace.

'Go!' he shouted at Ella. 'Run!'

'I can't leave you!'

'You have to!' He struggled against the machine, its sensors pulsing faster now. 'Find Doctor Santos!'

More skittering sounds approached. Ella stood frozen, torn between helping and running.

'Please,' Ash said. His eyes met hers, desperate and determined. 'You're too important. Go!'

With a sob, Ella turned and fled. Behind her, she heard Ash scream – once, twice, then silence.

She ran until her legs gave out, until her vision blurred with tears and exhaustion. When she stopped, slumping against a tunnel wall, she realised she had no idea where she was.

Lost in the dark, alone again. The story of her life, it seemed.

But now it was different. This time, people had died to protect her. Commander Chen, Amari, and Ash sacrificed everything because they believed she was important.

Because she'd survived the journey through time.

Ella pushed herself up, wiping her eyes. She couldn't let their sacrifices be for nothing. She had to find Doctor Santos and understand what was happening. She had to figure out why she was in this broken future and what it had to do with Elementals.

The tunnel stretched before her, dark and forbidding. Somewhere in the distance, she heard the skittering of mechanical legs.

Ella took a deep breath and started walking. One foot in front of the other. Keep moving. Stay alive.

Find answers.

The darkness swallowed her whole.

Chapter 3

The Key

Ella snapped awake in an underground bunker. It stank of damp stone and mould as she scrambled up, every inch of her screaming in agony. Electric lights flickered on the walls, casting ominous shadows everywhere. Had she stumbled into it and fallen asleep? She couldn't remember.

She sat against a wet wall and thought of home. Home. That word gnawed at her, as it had been doing each waking moment since she first opened her eyes in this alien-ravaged wasteland. She tightened her arms around her knees, trying to hold herself together. The hollow feeling in her chest hadn't left when she realised the truth — she was alone.

Her thoughts wandered back to her parents. Her mother's warm smile, her father's firm but gentle hands, and their reassuring presence. Gone. Her friends, too, vanished as if the earth had swallowed them up. All that remained was the broken memory of the island and then nothing but the cold, terrifying reality that she was trapped in a world that was no longer hers.

A lump formed in her throat as her mind replayed the

last moments she had with them — the chaos, the sinking feeling as the water enveloped her, the panic in her heart as everything disappeared. What if they were still out there, somewhere, imprisoned in this future like she was? Or worse — what if they were dead?

The walls of the bunker closed around her. Her breath quickened. She wanted to scream, to claw her way out of this nightmare, but her body refused to move. Exhaustion weighed her down, but her mind raced. She needed answers, something to hold on to. But all she had were questions.

And the others had sacrificed themselves for her – Amari, Ash, Commander Chen and the other people she'd seen.

'Ella?'

The voice shocked her into alertness. She jumped up, ready for a fight, even though all she wanted to do was collapse and sleep.

'Who?' she said.

A young woman stepped out of the shadows. 'You're safe, Ella. Don't you remember getting here? I'm Maia, and this is East Haven.'

Dirt and exhaustion lined Maia's face, but her eyes carried a glimmer of hope — hope Ella could no longer find in herself.

Then she remembered stumbling through the dark and finding others fleeing the alien attack. 'How long was I asleep?'

'A few hours,' Maia answered. 'We've got food ready if you're hungry.' Maia's voice was gentle, but Ella noticed the shadows under her eyes and the slight tremble in her hands.

Ella shook her head. 'I'm not hungry.' The truth was, she couldn't stomach the thought of eating. The grief sat heavy in her chest, taking up all the space her hunger should've filled.

Maia frowned but didn't push. 'I understand,' she said, sitting beside Ella on the rough stone floor. 'It's hard... I mean, all of this. Losing people.'

Ella's jaw clenched. 'You have no idea.'

'I lost my brother a few months ago,' Maia replied, her eyes distant. 'He was part of a scouting group. Got caught in an ambush by the invaders. We never found his body.'

Ella looked at her, feeling guilty and the slightest flicker of connection. She hadn't thought about the other people, how they might've suffered as much as she had. But it didn't make the pain any less. 'I'm sorry,' she whispered.

Maia offered a sad smile. 'We all lose someone in this world. It's what the invaders do. They take, and take, until there's nothing left. And then they take more.'

'Any news on the others?' Ella asked.

Maia shook her head. 'Not yet, but if anybody can get our people safe, it's Commander Chen.'

Ella's stomach churned with anger and grief, a bottomless pit of helplessness yawning wider inside her. 'I have to find a way home. I can't... I can't stay here. My parents, my friends... I don't even know if they're alive.'

Maia's smile faltered, her eyes growing sombre. 'You think you can get back to where you came from?'

'I have to try.'

Maia sat silent for a moment, her brow furrowing. Then she sighed. 'There are rumours... whispers, really. Among the resistance. They talk about an object the invaders have, something powerful.'

Ella turned her head. 'What do you mean?'

Maia glanced around, lowering her voice. 'I don't know all the details, but they call it the Key to Time. It's a device the invaders use. Some say it lets them see into the future. Others say it controls time itself. Either way, it's how they stay one step ahead of us, always knowing what we'll do before we do it.'

The words sent a jolt of something electric through Ella. The idea sounded impossible, but everything in this world felt impossible. 'Where is it?'

'Nobody knows for sure,' Maia said. 'But the resistance believes it's in their central hub, deep within the alien fortress. That's where they run the show — the labour camps, the patrols, the technology they use to keep us all in line.'

Ella's mind spun with the implications. If there was a device that controlled time... could it help her get back? Could she reverse everything, stop the invasion before it started, save her parents and friends from whatever fate had befallen them?

Her pulse quickened, a glimmer of hope piercing through the darkness suffocating her. 'How do I find it?'

Maia's eyes widened. 'You can't be thinking of going after it.'

'Why not?' Ella asked, her voice harder than she intended. 'If this thing exists and can control time, I must find it. I need to return to where I belong.'

Maia shook her head. 'Even if you could get inside the fortress — and that's a huge 'if' — it's suicide. No one has ever come back from there. The resistance has tried for years to breach it, but the invaders' technology is too advanced. They see everything coming before it happens.'

'I don't care,' Ella snapped, her voice sharp with desperation. 'If there's even the slightest chance this Key to Time can help me, I must try. I can't stay here. I won't lose them.'

Maia looked at her with pity and concern, her lips

pressing into a thin line. 'I get it, I do. But you're talking about going up against forces we don't understand. These invaders, their technology, their power — it's beyond us. And they don't just kill. They break people.'

Ella's breath hitched, but she forced herself to stand firm. She had to. 'I've lost everything. What else is there to take from me?'

Maia's eyes softened, studying Ella's face, perhaps recognising the determination or desperation that fuelled her.

'Doctor Santos might know more,' Maia said, standing up and brushing dirt off her pants. 'If you want to go after this thing, you'll need his help.'

Doctor Santos. She recalled Chen mentioning that name.

Find Doctor Santos!

Ella nodded, feeling the beginnings of a plan forming in her mind. 'Where is he?'

'There's a safe house further north,' Maia replied. 'It's dangerous to travel, but if you're serious about this, I'll take you there.'

Ella's throat tightened. 'Why would you help me?'

Maia paused, her eyes distant, before she looked at Ella. 'Because we've all lost someone. And if you think this Key to Time can make a difference, perhaps it's worth the risk.'

The two girls stood, the weight of the conversation hanging between them. Ella sensed something shift inside her, a spark of determination igniting the numbness that had gripped her since she woke up in her nightmare. Maybe this Key to Time was her only hope. Perhaps it was her only way home.

Maia broke the silence. 'Get some rest. We'll leave at first light.'

. . .

Ella lay in the corner of the bunker, staring at the rough-hewn stone ceiling as sleep evaded her. Her mind whirled with thoughts of the Key, of the invaders, of her parents' faces. She pictured them, frozen in time — her mother's soft eyes, her father's reassuring presence. She had to believe they were still out there, somewhere.

But what if they weren't? The thought gnawed at her, creeping into the cracks of her resolve. What if they were gone, lost in the waters that had swallowed her whole and spat her out into this broken world? What if she never found them again?

No. She couldn't think like that. Not now. Not when there was still a chance, however slim. She would find the Key and a way back to them.

And if that meant going into the heart of the alien stronghold, then so be it.

Her fingers clenched around the thin blanket Maia had given her. The chill in the air seeped through, but Ella didn't feel it. The cold inside her was deeper, rooted in loss and uncertainty. But that cold also fuelled her — a fire burning beneath it, a determination that refused to die.

Ella had always been a survivor. From the moment she learned who she was, from the day she discovered her connection to the Light, she'd faced danger, confronted fear, and kept going. This time would be no different. Tomorrow, she would embark on a new journey that could change everything. Or destroy everything.

But either way, she had to try.

For her parents. For her friends. For herself.

. . .

As the first light of dawn filtered into the bunker, casting weak shadows on the walls, Ella stood and prepared herself. Her body ached, her heart even more so, but the fire inside her had only grown. She glanced at Maia, who was gathering supplies for the journey ahead.

'Are you ready?' Maia asked, her voice low.

Ella nodded, her expression steeled. 'Let's go.'

Together, they slipped out of the bunker into the desolate world.

The weak sunshine painted the wasteland in shades of ash and bone. Ella's boots crunched on broken concrete as she followed Maia through the ruins. The air hung thick with an acrid smell that irritated her throat.

'Keep low,' Maia whispered, crouching behind a fallen wall. 'The drones are everywhere.'

Ella pressed herself against the cold stone, her heart hammering. 'How do they work?'

'Silent. Black. Like birds made of shadow.' Maia's voice carried a hint of carefully contained fear. 'They see in ways we don't understand: heat, movement, maybe even thoughts. The resistance lost thirty people last month when —' She cut herself off, pressing a finger to her lips.

A low hum filled the air, setting Ella's teeth on edge. She held her breath, watching as something dark passed overhead, its shape wrong in ways her mind couldn't quite process. The drone moved like a liquid shadow, its edges seeming to blur and shift.

The humming faded, but Ella's pulse didn't slow. She turned to Maia, who was studying her with an unreadable expression.

'You're different,' Maia said. 'The way you move, the way you watch things. You're not from any of the surviving colonies, are you?'

Her throat tightened. How much could she trust this stranger? But something in Maia's eyes – a hint of understanding, of shared pain – made her want to try.

'I'm from...' She swallowed hard. 'From before. Before all this.' The words felt inadequate, unable to capture the vast gulf between her world and this nightmare.

Maia's eyes widened, but she didn't look surprised. 'The rumours were true, then. About the time rifts.' She shifted closer, lowering her voice further. 'There were stories when the invasion first began. People appearing out of nowhere, talking about a different world. Most of them...' she trailed off, pain flickering across her face.

'What happened to them?' Ella asked.

'The invaders took them.' Maia's hands clenched. 'That's why we must be careful. If they realise what you are—'

A crash echoed from somewhere nearby, followed by the sound of shifting rubble. Both girls froze.

'We need to move,' Maia breathed.

They crept forward, staying in the shadows of the ruins. Ella's muscles burned from maintaining the crouch, but fear kept her moving. The morning light grew stronger, making her feel exposed. A glint of metal caught her eye – something half-buried in the debris. She paused, drawn to it despite herself. Reaching down, she brushed away the dust.

It was a child's toy robot, its chrome surface dulled and dented. Something about it made her chest ache. Had some kid dropped it while running?

'Ella.' Maia's urgent whisper snapped her back to the present. 'We can't stop.'

But Ella's fingers had found something else beneath the robot – a small notebook, its pages yellowed but intact. She tucked both items into her pocket, ignoring Maia's disapproving look.

They pressed on through the ruins, each step placed to avoid loose stones. Ella's mind kept returning to the toy robot, to the notebook. To all the little pieces of lost lives scattered around them.

'There,' Maia pointed to a collapsed building ahead. 'We can rest there for a minute. Check for patrols.'

It had once been some shop. Faded posters clung to the walls, advertising products from a world that no longer existed: exotic holidays, new gadgets and exciting toys. Ella gazed at them, trying to reconcile these fragments of normalcy with the apocalyptic landscape outside.

'You should eat something,' Maia said, offering a wrapped package. 'The safe house is still hours away.'

Ella took it, but her stomach rebelled at the thought of food. Instead, she pulled out the notebook she'd found. The cover was blank, but inside...

Her breath caught. The pages were filled with drawings – detailed sketches of machines. Each one annotated with observations, measurements, and weak points. The last few pages contained what looked like blueprints of some massive structure.

'Maia,' she whispered. 'Look at this.'

Maia moved closer, her expression changing as she saw the drawings. 'Someone from the resistance must have dropped this when...'

She didn't finish the sentence, but Ella knew what she meant.

When they were killed or taken.

'Somebody has been inside the alien fortress,' Ella said.

Maia sighed. 'Many people go inside the alien buildings, but none ever come out apart from the collaborators.'

'Collaborators?' Ella asked.

Maia spat into the dirt. 'Traitors – humans who betray their friends, neighbours, and families.'

Ella slipped the notebook into her pocket. 'Are there many of them?'

'Enough,' Maia replied. 'Too many. Come, we must keep moving.'

Ella wondered if her nightmare would ever end or if it was just beginning.

Chapter 4

Maia

Ella followed Maia in silence, the only sounds being the crunch of dirt beneath their feet and the distant hum of machines as they entered a forest. The day felt longer than usual; the sky washed in dull greys and oranges, casting an eerie glow over the ruined landscape. The alien structures loomed in the distance, metal monstrosities that clawed at the clouds, reflecting light like sharp, broken mirrors.

It had only been a few days since Ella had awakened in this desolate future, but it seemed like a lifetime. She was still getting used to the silence — a heavy, oppressive quiet that swallowed the world whole. Back home, there was always noise. The sound of birds, the chatter of people, the wind rustling through trees. Now, even the wind felt wrong, like it had been stifled by the weight of the invaders' presence.

'Ella?' Maia's voice broke through her thoughts.

Ella blinked, realising she'd been staring into the distance, lost in her mind. She looked at Maia, who was observing her. Concern was etched across her face, her dark eyes searching Ella's expression for something — a sign of hope. Or a sign of understanding.

'What?'

'Are you okay?' Maia asked.

Ella's first instinct was to lie. Tell her she was fine and could handle everything. But the truth was, she couldn't. She wasn't fine. Nothing about her current life was fine.

'I don't know,' Ella admitted.

The forest was dense, the trees twisted and gnarled, their bark scarred from years of war. The smell of damp earth and decay hung in the air.

'I get it,' Maia said, crossing her arms. 'It's a lot to take in. I felt the same way when I first woke up in this life. Being born into a world of occupiers isn't great.'

Ella frowned, still struggling to grasp everything that had happened. 'How did you...?' she trailed off, unsure how to finish the question. How had Maia survived? How had she kept going?

'How did I keep from losing my mind?' Maia finished for her, a small, sad smile tugging at the corner of her lips.

Ella nodded. 'Yes.'

Maia exhaled, glancing at the ground before answering. 'I didn't. Not at first. It was overwhelming. I lost my family, too. Everyone I knew. And for a long time, I didn't want to fight. I just wanted to find a way out. I needed to escape.'

Ella's chest tightened at the mention of family. She pictured her mother's face — her soft smile, how she always knew the right thing to say. Her father's strong arms wrapped around her in a hug, his voice calm and steady.

Now they were gone. Stuck in a past that Ella might never return to. And that's if they survived that sinking island. And The Soulless. And the Institute.

'I don't know if I can do this,' Ella said. She glanced at

Maia, her eyes shining with unshed tears. 'I don't know if I'm strong enough.'

'You don't have to be strong always,' Maia replied. 'None of us are. But you have to keep going. Even when it feels impossible.'

Ella looked away, her throat tightening with emotion. She didn't want to cry. But the weight of everything pressed down on her, and she wasn't sure how long she could hold it together.

'I'm not like you,' Ella said. 'I'm not a soldier.'

Maia stepped closer, touching Ella's arm. 'Neither was I. None of us were, not at first. We were just people trying to survive. But then we realised that if we didn't fight, we wouldn't survive.'

Ella's mind raced with conflicting emotions. She wanted to believe Maia and trust she could find the strength to keep going. But every instinct in her screamed to turn back, to run away from everything. She wasn't ready to face a war, unprepared to lose herself in a fight she didn't understand.

But where would she run to?

'I don't know if I can do this,' she repeated.

Maia studied Ella for a long moment, her expression softening with understanding.

'You've already survived more than most people could. You woke up in a ruined world, and you're still here. That's something.'

Ella shook her head, her mind swirling with doubt. 'But what if I'm not strong enough? What if I fail?'

Maia smiled. 'We all fail, Ella. But it's not about being perfect or always winning. It's about trying and not giving up, even when everything is against you.'

Ella's heart ached. She wanted to believe that. She

hoped she could keep going, fight back against the invaders and somehow, some way, return to her family. Yet the fear was still there, gnawing at her insides like a relentless tide. What if the aliens killed her? What if she never saw her parents again? She reached deep inside her, trying to find the Light she'd once had. If she could recover what she'd taken from Pandora in the multiverse, then maybe she could use it to defeat the aliens.

But there was nothing there, only a faint echo keeping her going. She'd used everything to defeat Lyssa. And for what? For this desolate future?

She leaned against a tree, desperate to catch her breath.

'We'll rest for an hour,' Maia said.

Ella didn't argue, slumping into the grass. She reached into her bag and removed the water bottle Maia had given her earlier. Ella sipped on it, knowing she had to keep more for later, even though her body cried out to drink it all.

'What do the aliens look like?' Ella asked.

Maia drank from her bottle, chewing on bread. 'Like us, but yellow.'

'Yellow?'

Maia nodded. 'Their skin. It glistens when the sun hits them, though I've only seen one from a distance. They don't come into human lands – they send their machines for that.'

Ella shivered. 'Do you know this Doctor Santos?'

'Only by reputation.'

'What type of doctor is he?'

Maia shrugged. 'No idea.' She closed her eyes. 'Get some rest.'

Ella tried.

But there were too many nightmares.

· · ·

Later that evening, they reached the resistance's hideout. Hidden beneath the ruins of an old industrial complex, the underground bunker was a maze of concrete tunnels and dark chambers. It stank of oil and sweat, very different from the open fields and forests Ella remembered from the island.

The resistance fighters moved quietly, their faces drawn and weary. Most of them were older than Ella, their eyes hardened by years of war and loss. They acknowledged Maia, but most didn't give Ella a second look.

Ella felt out of place. What could she do to help them? She had no weapons, no Light and had lost the Book of All Life and the other artefacts she'd had on the island.

She didn't belong there. She wasn't like them.

'You're Ella, right?' A voice pulled her from her thoughts.

Ella turned to see a young man standing nearby. His hair was short and messy, his clothes worn and patched in several places. His eyes, though sharp, held a hint of curiosity.

'Yeah,' Ella replied. 'That's me.'

'I'm Drax. Maia told us about you. Said you're not from around here. You lost your memory?'

Ella shook his hand, feeling the roughness of his calloused skin. 'Something like that.'

Drax studied her, his gaze lingering on her face as if he were trying to piece together her story. 'Must be strange, waking up in a world like this.'

Ella laughed. 'That's one way to put it.'

Drax smiled, though there was no humour in it. 'I've been here long enough to forget what it used to be like, what my parents told me about the world before. I guess it's easier like that.'

Ella's chest tightened. She didn't want to forget. She

didn't want to let go of the memories of her mum and dad, her friends, and her home. But she recognised the truth in Drax's eyes — the longer she stayed in this world, the harder it would be to hold on to the past.

'Maia said you're not sure about joining us,' Drax added. 'That you're still trying to figure things out.'

Ella glanced at Maia, who was talking to a group of fighters. 'I'm not a soldier. I just want to get home.'

Drax nodded. 'I understand that. We all want something we've lost. But the truth is, home doesn't exist anymore. Not the way it used to.'

Ella's stomach churned. She didn't want to believe that. She couldn't. Her family and friends were still out there, somewhere, waiting for her if she could find a way back.

'Look, I won't lie to you,' Drax continued, his voice low. 'This fight is brutal. It's messy and doesn't always feel like we're winning. But we keep going because we have to. Because if we don't, then everything we've lost and suffered through, it'll all be for nothing.'

Ella bit her lip. She understood what he was saying. She saw the conviction in his eyes, the fire that kept him pushing forward even when the odds were against him. But she wasn't sure if she had that same fire.

'Just think about it,' Drax said, giving her a slight nod before walking away.

She watched him leave, her heart heavy with uncertainty. She knew what he was asking of her — what Maia was asking. They wanted her to join the resistance, to fight alongside them in a war that felt impossible to win.

But all Ella wanted was to go home. To see her family again.

And to do that, she'd have to fight.

Chapter 5

The Doctor

Ella leaned against the damp wall of the underground chamber, listening to the steady drip of water echoing through the bunker's stale air. Her head buzzed with questions, and the tension in the room seemed to thicken as the man opposite her studied her. Doctor Santos looked nothing like she'd expected—older than most of the resistance fighters, with wiry grey hair, a worn face, and a scar that ran from his cheek to his jawline. His hands were calloused, fingers wrapped around a strange metal device that pulsed with faint blue light.

'You're Ella,' he said, breaking the silence at last.

Ella nodded. 'And you're Doctor Santos. Maia mentioned you might have answers.'

Santos's gaze flicked to Maia, who stood just behind Ella, silent and tense. 'She's right. I know things that most people here don't. About the invaders, their tech, their fortress.' He paused, letting his words sink in, his face shadowed with grim certainty. 'But I'll warn you now, child. The answers won't be what you want to hear.'

Ella crossed her arms, the chill of the bunker pressing

in. 'I've been hearing that a lot.' She kept her tone light, but there was an edge to it—a bitterness that surprised even her. 'Everyone tells me what I can't do, but nobody's giving me a way forward.'

'Sometimes,' Santos replied, 'knowing the limits can be the only path forward.'

Ella's jaw tightened. 'I didn't come here to learn my limits.'

'Then tell me what you came here for,' he challenged.

Ella opened her mouth to answer, but hesitated. What had she come for? To survive, sure, but it was more than that—she wanted her family, her world back. She wanted everything the invaders had taken from her. How could she put that into words?

'I want to know how to get back,' she said. 'How to fix this—to return to my family and friends. I don't belong here.'

He clasped his hands together. 'So, you think you came here from fifty years ago, that you travelled through time?'

Ella hadn't wanted to admit that to any of them, but knew she had no choice if she was to find a way back to 2025.

'Yes,' she said. 'It sounds crazy, but that's what happened.'

Santos placed the metallic object on the table. 'Ever since the invaders arrived, all I've dealt with is craziness. So, tell me your story.'

She did, right from the beginning and finding the Book of All Life on Saltburn cliffs in what seemed a lifetime ago.

'We were on the island in the North Sea – my mum and dad and friends – fighting The Soulless and the Institute when the earth shattered around us and the island sank. I was in the water one second, and the next, I was here.

That's why I need to return home, to travel back in time to before any of this happened.'

A flicker of something—sympathy?—crossed Santos's face, but it was gone before Ella could be sure. 'There may be a way,' he said, his voice low, almost reverent. 'But it's more dangerous than anything you can imagine. This isn't a journey you just walk into.'

She sighed with relief. 'You believe me?'

He nodded. 'I do.'

Ella's eyes sharpened. 'Tell me how I can go home.'

Santos shifted in his seat. 'The invaders have a device— a machine that can see the future. We call it the Key to Time, though I doubt that's its true name. It's ancient, older than any human civilisation. And it's the reason they're always ahead of us.'

'A machine that sees the future?' Ella repeated, a shiver running through her. She glanced at Maia, whose expression was unreadable, eyes fixed on Santos. 'How did you hear of this device?'

'We had spies inside their main fortress who brought us the information.' His face darkened. 'The aliens feed it using human sacrifices. Our people.' His voice trembled with disgust. 'We lose fighters, only to find out later that they've been taken, their life force drained to fuel that device.'

Ella's stomach churned. 'But why? How does it work?'

Santos shook his head. 'No one knows. We only know it has a hunger for human energy. That's why the invaders take people from the labour camps, why they sweep the city's ruins and snatch anyone unlucky enough to be caught.'

'So, it's inside their fortress?' she asked.

'Yes. At the heart of it,' Santos replied. 'Protected by

walls, sentries, drones, and forces that would tear any human intruder apart before they even got close.'

She clenched her fists. Every answer left her with more questions, each one gnawing at her more than the last. 'How can we fight back if they see every move before we make it?'

Santos's gaze softened. 'That's the problem. There is no way to fight it. The resistance has tried everything. Some of our best fighters made it close to where the object is, but none ever returned.'

Ella swallowed the frustration rising within her. 'So, you're saying it's impossible to get inside?'

'Not and survive,' he replied. 'But maybe—'

'I'll find a way.' Her voice was stern, brittle. She stood, resisting the urge to lash out. 'Thank you, Doctor Santos, but I'm not staying here. I can't wait for something to change.'

He watched her, the weight of his gaze like a magnet refusing to let her go. 'I've seen the results from the scan our colleagues made of you before the attack on the bunker.' His gaze cut into her. 'You're human, but different.'

'And?'

'You might be what the invaders have been looking for?'

Ella narrowed her eyes. 'Looking for?'

He nodded. 'Yes. As I mentioned, you're different from other people.'

She smiled. 'My parents always told me that.' She turned to Maia, who had been standing like a statue, listening to every word. 'I need to go. I can't stay here.'

Maia's eyes softened. 'Then let me come with you.'

'Maia,' Santos said, 'you know what you'd be risking—'

'I understand,' Maia interrupted. She moved to Ella's side, her hand resting on her shoulder. 'But if there's a chance—however small—that Ella can do this, I'll help her.'

Santos's face twisted in frustration, but he didn't argue. 'Then go, but don't mention it to anybody else. There is already talk of keeping you here, Ella.'

Ella dug her nails into her palms. 'As a prisoner?'

'As our guest,' he replied. 'Until we know more about you.'

She peered deep into his eyes. 'Do you know what Elementals are?'

He shook his head. 'No.'

'Commander Chen mentioned the Elemental Purge. Have you heard of that?'

'No,' he repeated.

She didn't believe him.

Ella turned to leave.

As Doctor Santos leaned forward, his face fell into shadow. 'Before you go, there's something you need to see. Come with me.'

Ella glanced at Maia, whose eyes flickered with apprehension. They followed Santos through a series of dark, narrow passageways, winding deeper into the underground bunker, away from the murmurs and movements of the other resistance members. A strange smell lingered in the air, a mix of chemicals and something metallic, an aroma that made Ella's stomach clench.

They stopped before a thick metal door, its surface dented and rusted around the edges. Santos hesitated before pressing a series of numbers into a keypad. The entrance slid open with a grinding sound, revealing a room cast in dim, flickering light. A powerful stench hit Ella—a sickly sweet rot that tightened her throat. She pressed her sleeve to her nose, trying not to gag.

'What's this?' she said.

Santos stepped inside, gesturing for them to follow. 'I

warned you. The answers you're searching for won't be easy to accept.'

The room had metal tables lined against the walls, each holding something covered in a grey, stained cloth. The shapes underneath were unmistakable—human-like, but off, too long, too thin in some places, almost distorted. Ella's skin prickled as she stepped closer, her heart hammering against her ribs.

Santos pulled the material back from one body, revealing the alien beneath. Its flesh was a muted, glistening yellow, stretched tight over a bony frame that was both delicate and sturdy. Its limbs were long, fingers tapering into piercing, dark points. Its eyes were hollow—large, almond-shaped, and black as coal, staring into nothingness.

Ella shivered. She forced herself to look, to take in every detail. The face was angular, with high cheekbones and thin lips that pulled back, revealing sharp, pointed teeth. The entire body seemed to have an eerie symmetry, as if it had been crafted rather than born.

She stepped away, swallowing against the bile rising in her throat. 'Is this...?'

'An invader,' Santos confirmed. 'We were lucky to retrieve it after a patrol caught one off-guard, though we lost two fighters to get it here. They don't come into our areas without their machines or sentries. But we need to know what we're fighting.'

Ella studied the alien's form as though memorising it would give her some insight. The creature appeared almost human, yet every part exuded a sense of wrongness, an instinctual discomfort that made her skin crawl.

'Why keep them here?' she asked. 'What do you hope to learn?'

'We've been studying them for years, but their biology

defies our understanding. It's not just that they look different; they're built for something beyond this world. Faster reflexes and heightened strength. They're superior to us in every way. And then there's this.'

Santos pointed to a mark on the creature's neck—a dark, tattoo-like emblem burned into its yellow skin. It resembled a twisted, looping symbol Ella couldn't place, yet she felt a jolt of familiarity. It almost seemed to pulse under the dim light, its edges glowing as if alive.

'What is it?' she whispered, reaching to touch it but stopping short.

'We think it's connected to their device, the one they use to see into the future,' Santos replied. 'Each alien we've seen up close bears this mark. We suspect it's how they communicate, how they share information with the device, perhaps even relay messages to each other.'

Horror and fascination swirled within Ella. The machine, the sacrifices, the resistance fighters who'd never returned—every part of this invasion felt deliberate, precise, like a trap laid out long ago, now tightening around the remnants of humanity.

'And this machine,' she said. 'You're certain it's real?'

Santos's gaze turned sharp. 'More real than you want it to be. We've lost countless people trying to stop it, to damage it—anything. But no one has ever come back.'

The importance of his words settled over her, cold and unrelenting. She peered at the alien's lifeless form, the black eyes staring through her. She felt exposed, vulnerable, as though it could see her every weakness.

'How did they get here?' she asked.

'They come from beyond our understanding,' he answered. 'And whatever they want here, it's worth any cost to them. Their machine requires human energy, and they're willing to tear down everything to get it.'

Nausea twisted in Ella's stomach. The smell, the eerie stillness of the alien, the horror of what she'd learned—it was all pressing in, suffocating her. 'I need to leave.'

Without waiting for a response, she turned and rushed out of the room, ignoring the concerned looks from the other resistance fighters as she pushed past them. She didn't stop until she reached a corridor, where she doubled over, hands on her knees, gasping for air.

Maia's footsteps echoed behind her. She approached Ella, her gaze filled with understanding. 'It's not easy, seeing them up close.'

Ella straightened, rubbing a hand over her face. 'They're like us, but so twisted, so wrong.' She shivered, the image of those hollow black eyes lingering in her mind. 'And that machine they have...if it sees the future, then we're fighting a losing battle, aren't we?'

Maia's expression softened, but there was a hardness in her gaze, a fire Ella hadn't seen before. 'Maybe. But we can't stop. We're all that's left. We must fight, even if we can't see the end.'

Ella looked at her, searching Maia's face for any sign of doubt, but there was none. 'Then help me. Help me get close to it. I have to try. If there's any chance of getting inside that fortress, of stopping them...'

Maia nodded, a faint smile touching her lips. 'I'll get you there. Whatever it takes.'

As they left behind the horrors of the mortuary, the determination in Ella's heart grew. The memory of those lifeless eyes, of the alien's twisted form, lingered in her mind like a shadow. She wouldn't let that image haunt her forever. She would face the machine and stop it.

She and Maia climbed the narrow, winding stairs back up to the ruined city, the echoes of the underground fading with each step. The air outside was thick and humid, pressing in on them as they left the resistance's hideout and travelled through the dense maze of the city. The towering alien fortress loomed in the distance, a dark, foreboding structure that seemed to pulse with an unholy energy.

Ella shivered as she studied the jagged, twisted metal that formed its skeleton, rising like a black scar against the horizon. Maia walked beside her, eyes alert, her expression a mixture of caution and determination. They moved in silence, each lost in their thoughts until Maia broke the quiet.

'You could turn back and survive with the resistance.'

Ella was surprised by the statement. 'My family and friends - if there's a way to save them or just to know what happened, I must try. Even if it means going into that fortress.'

And not coming back out.

Maia nodded, a flicker of sadness crossing her face. 'I understand. I lost my brother a while back. It's the not knowing that eats at you.'

They continued in silence, the tension between them thick with unspoken fears. As they moved deeper into the city, the crumbling buildings rose like skeletal remains on either side, broken windows glinting in the low light. The only sounds were the distant hum of alien drones and the scuttling of creatures hiding in the shadows.

Ella's lips trembled, scanning the streets, every shadow and sound setting her nerves on edge. She glanced at Maia, who was tense, alert to each movement. 'What's out here?'

'Everything,' Maia replied. 'Wild animals, scavengers, desperate people. None of them friendly.'

Ella swallowed hard, the hairs on her neck prickling. 'So we're just hoping they don't find us?'

'Pretty much. Welcome to survival in the alien apocalypse.'

They continued, keeping to the shadows, weaving through alleys and backstreets, never staying in one place too long. But even in the quiet, there was a constant, gnawing sense of danger, as if unseen eyes were watching their every move.

The sun was dipping below the horizon when they stopped to rest near an old, broken-down building. Ella leaned against the wall, catching her breath, and Maia handed her a piece of stale bread, her gaze scrutinising their surroundings.

'How much farther?' Ella asked, her voice weary.

Maia shrugged. 'Hard to say. We'll get as close as we can tonight and rest. We'll need our strength for whatever's waiting.'

Ella nodded, chewing the dry bread, each bite a painful reminder of how far she was from the world she'd known. She pictured her parents sitting at the kitchen table, laughing as they shared a meal. The thought sent a pang of longing through her, but she pushed it away, forcing herself to focus on the present. A rustling sound caught her attention, and she stiffened. Maia's eyes flicked to her, alert and cautious.

'Stay close,' Maia whispered, her hand on the hilt of her knife. She gestured toward a doorway, and Ella followed as quietly as possible.

The rustling grew louder, replaced by a low growl that echoed off the walls. Ella pressed herself against the doorway. Maia crouched beside her, studying the darkness. A large, dark shape emerged from the shadows—a dog, but leaner, wilder, its eyes gleaming with a feral hunger. Its fur was matted, and the hound moved with a predatory grace, sniffing the air.

Ella held her breath, her pulse racing. The dog moved closer, its gaze fixed on her, lips curling back to reveal sharp teeth.

Maia raised a hand, signalling her to stay still. She reached for a stone on the ground and tossed it to the side, drawing the dog's attention. It darted toward the noise, growling as it searched for the source.

'Now,' Maia whispered, tugging Ella's arm.

They slipped away, rushing through the maze of crumbling walls. Ella's heart hammered as they put distance between themselves and the dog, the weight of the danger pressing around them.

When they were a safe distance, Maia slowed, glancing back to make sure they hadn't been followed. 'Always be aware of your surroundings. Everything here is hungry.'

Ella nodded, a shaky breath escaping her. 'Thanks. I...I didn't see it coming.'

'Few do.' Maia's voice softened, a hint of sympathy in her tone. 'But you learn fast in this world, or you don't last.'

They continued, each step taking them closer to the alien fortress. As they navigated the ruins, they passed through pockets of life—stray animals, desperate people huddled around small fires, their eyes hollow and haunted. Some called out, begging for food or shelter, but Maia kept them moving, her face set in a grim mask.

'You can't save everyone,' she said when Ella shot her a questioning look. 'The more you give, the more they'll take. Out here, it's every person for themselves.'

Ella's chest tightened, a wave of guilt washing over her as she looked back at the people they'd left behind. She wanted to help, to do something for them, but Maia's words echoed in her mind. She couldn't save everyone.

The alien structure loomed ahead when they reached the city's edge, a monstrous silhouette against the darkening sky. It pulsed with an eerie energy, casting an unnerving glow that sent shivers down Ella's spine.

'This is it,' Maia murmured. 'The fortress.'

Ella stared at the towering structure floating high above the ground, her heart pounding. She glanced at Maia, who was watching her, eyes filled with caution and trust.

'It's defying gravity,' Ella said.

Maia nodded. 'Alien tech.'

Ella removed the notebook from her pocket. 'This might help me get inside.'

'You don't have to do this,' Maia replied, her voice gentle yet firm. 'No one would blame you for turning back.'

Ella thought of her family, her friends, everything she'd lost. She couldn't stop now.

'I'm going.'

She'd get home, no matter what.

Chapter 6

The Stranger

Ella studied the floating alien construction. The metallic structure hovered in the sky, a dark mass of twisting machinery and glowing lights, suspended as if gravity had lost its grip. She'd seen plenty of strange things before, but nothing like this. It didn't belong in her world, a grotesque scar on the landscape, a permanent reminder that everything had changed.

Her breath fogged in the cold, her fingers stiff despite the thin leather gloves she wore. The sky was a dull grey, blending into the horizon where the massive hovering compound loomed, a dark shadow in the air that distorted the view with its pulsing lights. It didn't seem real. Like a nightmare pulled from the recesses of her mind, it drifted above the city's ruins. Now, it was all broken concrete, shattered windows, and the skeletal remains of buildings clawing upward like desperate hands.

'We need to find a way in,' Ella said. She hadn't realised she'd spoken aloud until Maia glanced back, walking ahead.

'Nothing in that notebook?' Maia asked.

Ella gripped the book before throwing it down. 'No. I've

looked through it several times, and there's no mention of an access point, just diagrams of machinery.'

Maia's jaw tightened. 'We need information from someone inside.'

Ella blinked. 'From a traitor? A collaborator?'

'Yes,' Maia answered. 'I can't think of another option.'

Ella gazed at the floating structure – she didn't know why, but it terrified her like nothing else had since arriving in that forsaken future. She'd fought Elementals – harpies, dragons, and other weird beasts – and had even stood against The Soulless and the Institute, but this alien *thing* was different.

Then, there was her ancestor, Pandora, the Goddess of all creation. Ella had drained Pandora of the source of her power – the Light that existed in all creatures but especially in Elementals – but nothing was left in her now, extinguished long before she sunk with that island. She hadn't mentioned this to Maia or the others, assuming they would think she was crazy.

Ella wondered what had happened to her Elemental friends – Seraphina, Barbara, Peg and the others – supposing they lived longer than humans and should be around somewhere. Unless this wasn't her Earth but a duplicate, part of the multiverse. She'd fallen into the multiverse before. Was she in it again? Was Pandora here?

She shivered at the thought. Pandora. Ella had left her powerless in the multiverse, but that was over fifty years ago. Still, you can't kill a god. And what was the Elemental Purge Commander Chen had mentioned, and Doctor Santos had lied about not knowing?

Ella gazed at the alien structure again, marvelling at how it floated above the ground. Had Pandora created these aliens?

She kicked a stray rock as they walked. 'It feels like we're always watching and doing nothing.'

'You're not ready to do anything yet,' Maia said, cutting through Ella's words. 'We've talked about this.'

Ella's jaw clenched, but she kept her mouth shut. She knew she wasn't ready. She didn't need Maia to remind her of that. The reality was, she wasn't sure if she'd ever be prepared. Not in this broken world that wasn't hers. The real truth she couldn't say out loud was that she didn't want to get involved. She wanted to find another way out, a different path home.

Maia pulled her scarf tighter around her neck. 'We could wait here until we see someone leave.'

'Yeah,' Ella replied, though her voice lacked conviction. Her hands shook, and not just from the cold. 'And then what?'

'We have to figure out what the aliens are doing here,' Maia explained. 'They're always moving their compounds, shifting locations. But this one has been here for weeks, which means something's going on. We need to know what.'

Ella nodded, though she wasn't sure how useful she would be. She still felt like a puzzle piece that didn't quite fit.

As they descended the rocky path toward the valley, the compound grew larger in the sky, casting a massive shadow over the barren land below. The sound of alien machinery hummed, a low, vibrating noise that made Ella want to throw up. She sensed the presence of the invaders, even though they were still a mile away.

'What do you think it's like inside?' Ella said, breaking the silence as they walked.

Maia shot her a glance. 'Inside the compound? You don't want to know.'

Ella bit her lip, realising she'd struck a nerve. She'd heard stories about the alien compounds — places where human prisoners were experimented on, where the invaders conducted their research in secret. But hearing about it was one thing. Seeing the fortress made it all too real.

Then something hit her like a wave—invisible fingers squeezing her heart, an awareness she couldn't explain. They weren't alone.

Ella grabbed Maia's arm, stopping her mid-step. 'Wait.'

Maia's eyes narrowed, but before she could say anything, a figure emerged from behind the jagged remains of a wall. It was subtle initially, a slight movement that caught Ella's eye, but it was enough. A cloaked being, tall and strange, moved into view as if they'd been watching, waiting for the right moment to reveal themselves.

'Who the hell—' Maia started, reaching for her weapon.

Ella's pulse pounded in her ears, her throat tightening as she froze. The figure wasn't human. The glow of their skin in the compound's shadow made that clear. They stepped forward, hands raised, a gesture that spoke of surrender or peace, but it didn't ease the knot of tension in Ella's chest.

'Don't be afraid,' it said.

'Stop,' Maia replied. 'One more step, and I'll shoot.'

The intruder stopped, hands still raised. Their voice was quiet, soft, almost melodic. 'I'm not your enemy.'

'Yeah, I've heard that before,' Maia snapped. She inched forward, her focus never leaving the stranger. 'Who are you? Why are you here?'

The figure moved its hood an inch, revealing pale, glowing yellow skin and eyes that shimmered like a distant star. Ella gasped – this was a live alien. She peered at the twisted, looping symbol on its neck, unable to look away.

'My name is Aelix,' they said. 'I'm here to help you.'

Maia scoffed, her grip on the gun tightening. 'Help us? You're one of them.'

'I was,' Aelix corrected, their gaze flickering between Maia and Ella. 'Not anymore. Lower your weapon. I'm here to help.'

Maia didn't budge. 'Why should we trust you?'

'Because I've seen what's inside that compound,' the alien replied, nodding toward the floating structure in the distance. 'And I know what they're planning.'

Ella stepped forward. 'What do you mean?'

The alien glanced at her, their glowing eyes meeting hers before they spoke again. 'They're using it to monitor time. They have a device, something we call the Key. It allows them to manipulate events to stay ahead of any resistance. That's why you can never win.'

'Why should we trust you?' Ella asked, her voice stronger.

The alien hesitated, then pulled back their hood, revealing their face. Their features were sharp and angular, with pale, glowing skin and eyes that gleamed in the dim light. But there was something human in their expression, a softness Ella recognised.

'I'm not one of them,' Aelix said. 'Not anymore.'

Ella stared at Aelix, her mind racing. Up close, their yellow skin shimmered, catching the weak sunlight filtering through the clouds, but there was a haunted look in their eyes as if they carried the weight of countless horrors. The looping symbol on Aelix's neck pulsed, and though they were an alien, something about their expression tugged at Ella's instincts. She knew fear and desperation and saw both in how Aelix held their hands and the tense line of their shoulders.

'Not anymore?' Maia echoed, her tone dripping with

suspicion. 'You think you can just show up here, drop a few vague promises, and we'll trust you?'

'I don't expect trust,' Aelix replied, lowering their hands. Their soft and smooth voice contained a strange undercurrent, as if every word was chosen carefully. 'But if you go into that fortress without understanding what's inside, you won't last a second. I can assist you in bypassing their defences and help you understand the Key.'

Ella's eyes shifted between Maia and Aelix, the hairs on her neck still tingling. 'Why would you betray them? Why turn against them now?'

Aelix hesitated, their gaze dropping for the briefest moment. 'I've seen things. Things not easy to unsee. They may look like me, but they're nothing like me. The machine —' They broke off, their jaw tightening as if holding back the memory of some dark, unshakable truth.

'What does it do?' Ella's voice was quiet, but the question cut through the tension.

Aelix's eyes flicked to her as if gauging how much she could handle. 'It doesn't just see the future. It warps it. The Key is attuned to human minds. Every time it connects to one of you, it saps away part of their essence, creating pathways—variations of events. The machine alters probabilities to ensure their dominance and keep them a step ahead of you.'

'Attuned to...human minds?' Ella's stomach turned. She remembered Doctor Santos's words and the dead alien. 'You mean it works off human sacrifices?'

'Yes,' Aelix said, their face shadowed with guilt. 'And they'll use it until there's nothing left to take. They believe they're untouchable. But I know a way you can destroy it.'

Maia's face darkened, but her grip on her weapon loosened. 'And what would that be?'

'Human hands can't touch it,' Aelix continued, stepping closer. 'The Key's shield responds only to our kind, to the markers they placed on us.' They pointed to the strange symbol on their neck. 'If I go with you, I can get you close, past the sentries, the barriers...to the core.'

Ella's eyes widened, her imagination racing with fear and hope. 'And then what? Even if you get us there, how do we destroy it?'

Aelix's expression held a glimmer of something Ella couldn't identify—regret, maybe, or sorrow. 'That part...I don't know for certain. The Key isn't just a machine; it's connected to something...deeper. Something that draws from this world and others. But I know it has a weakness, a flaw built to stabilise it. Perhaps we can find that weakness together if I get you inside.'

Maia narrowed her eyes. 'Why would you help us if it means your people will come after you?'

'Because I'm tired,' Aelix replied, their voice almost a whisper. 'Tired of being part of something that devours everything it touches. I thought I could ignore it, that I could just...exist. But the cost—' They swallowed, looking down. 'The cost is too great. I don't want to see another world burn.'

Ella gasped. 'They've done this to other planets?'

Aelix nodded. 'Hundreds. My people have built an empire across the universe on this thing they found floating in space centuries ago.'

Ella felt the weight of their words. She thought of her family, her friends, and the countless lives lost. She studied Aelix's face, watching for any sign of deception, but all she saw was a hollow, broken resignation.

'If you help us,' Ella said, 'what's to stop them from tracking us down?'

'They don't know I'm here,' Aelix replied, glancing over their shoulder as if expecting to see shadows in the mist. 'But they will eventually. They're relentless. If you agree, we'll need to move quickly.'

Maia's lips tightened, the conflict clear in her eyes. She looked at Ella. 'This is a trap.' She glared at Aelix. 'You think this *creature* appears here by accident, just where we are?'

Ella understood, but something inside her pulled toward Aelix. It was a risk, a terrible one, but it was also the first real chance since she'd woken up in this strange world. 'I know. But it's a risk we have to take. We don't have any other choice. We weren't just going to stroll into that place, were we?'

Maia stared at her for a moment, then took a slow breath. 'Fine.' She lowered her weapon but kept a wary eye on Aelix. 'But if you so much as twitch wrong, alien, I'll shoot you.'

Aelix didn't flinch, nodding in quiet acceptance. 'I understand.'

Later, they huddled around a small fire deep in a cave for shelter. The heat of the flames did little to ease the chill that had settled into Ella's bones. She sat cross-legged on the ground, her arms folded across her chest as Aelix told their story.

'I was part of the first wave from our planet, Thelxon,' Aelix said, staring into the fire. 'Not all of us wanted this,' they continued, their voice softer, tinged with regret. 'Some of us believed in coexistence, in sharing this world. But others desired control. They didn't trust humans.'

Maia snorted. 'Smart.'

Aelix glanced at her, but there was no anger in their eyes. 'It wasn't about intelligence. It was fear. Fear that humans would reject us, fight us. So, they took control. Forced it.'

Ella watched the flames dance, her mind half in the present, half somewhere else—somewhere far away. Aelix's words echoed in her head, but she could only think about her family. Her parents. Her friends. Did they even exist anymore? Had they lived out their lives oblivious to the horrors that were unfolding in this future? Or had the invasion destroyed everything she once knew? Part of her wanted this not to be her Earth. But would that make it harder to return home?

She swallowed the lump in her throat. 'What changed for you?'

Aelix's eyes met hers, and Ella recognised something she hadn't expected—guilt. 'I saw what we were doing, what we were becoming. It wasn't what I'd signed up for. I couldn't watch it anymore.'

'What did you see?' Maia asked, her tone harsh, but Ella heard the curiosity beneath the surface.

Aelix's hands tightened around the edges of their cloak. 'The experiments. Torture. Murder. And how they use the Key.'

The Key.

'What does it do?' Ella asked.

Aelix's gaze shifted to her, their expression unreadable. 'It allows them to see time. Multiple timelines. They can predict what will happen and adjust their actions.'

Ella's stomach twisted. 'So they see the future?'

'Not exactly,' Aelix said, shaking their head. 'It's more complex than that. They see potential futures and different possibilities. It's why you can never win. Every time you move, they know what's coming.'

Maia cursed under her breath. 'So, what? We're screwed?'

Aelix's expression darkened. 'Not necessarily. The Key is powerful, but it's also dangerous. If misused, it could unravel everything.'

'You mentioned multiple timelines,' Ella said. 'Potential futures and different possibilities.' Aelix nodded. 'Does that mean other Earths exist alongside this one?'

'It's possible,' Aelix replied. 'But either way, you can never gain the upper hand. Every time you fight back, they've already seen what's coming and have a plan ready to deal with you.'

'So how do we stop them?' Ella asked.

Aelix hesitated. 'It's not simple. The Key is powerful, but it's also dangerous. If you tamper with time and try to change things, the consequences could be catastrophic.'

Ella's stomach twisted. She thought of what she'd lost. Could the Key be the solution? Could it take her back to the past, to the world she knew?

But Aelix's warning echoed in her mind. Dangerous. Catastrophic.

'What do you mean?' Ella said.

Aelix met her gaze. 'If you use the Key to change time, you could unravel everything. The future, the past, it could all collapse. There's no way to know for sure what will happen.'

Ella struggled to breathe. She wanted to go back to fix everything.

But at what cost?

Chapter 7

Resistance

The wind cut through Ella's jacket as she stood on the edge of the ruins, staring at the alien structure. The sky was dark, obscured by thick clouds that seemed to mirror the weight in her chest. The breeze tugged at her hair, carrying the scent of death. Below, the remains of the city sprawled out, the skeletal ruins of what had once been a thriving metropolis. Now, it was only rubble and wreckage overrun by invading forces. Giant mechanical structures dotted the horizon, hovering above the ground.

Aelix stood a few steps behind her. 'I apologise for everything *my* people have done to yours.' They sighed. 'Now, this is it. Once you cross that line, there's no going back.'

The weight of Aelix's words hung heavy in the air between them. She'd resisted becoming involved, hoping for another way to return to her family without throwing herself into an impossible war. But that hope had faded, replaced by the harsh reality of this broken world. She pictured her parents, their faces blurry in her memory, like a dream she couldn't quite recall. She thought of her friends, the life she'd once known. It was so far away, and the only chance of returning to it lay in the heart of the alien stronghold.

Aelix was right. Once she made this choice, there was no turning back.

The decision to join the resistance had been gnawing at her since she stepped foot in this future. People had sacrificed themselves for her – Amari, Ash, Commander Chen and countless others. And for what? So she could take on the impossible task of getting inside the alien compound and then trying to use an alien artefact – this Key to Time – to do what? Take her home and leave this world in ruins to the invaders?

No – to change time and stop this from ever happening.

Then what? What will happen to all those who were born after the alien invasion? Would they just snap out of existence if she returned home?

Every part of her screamed to find another way—to avoid this impossible mission. But there was no other way, was there? The Key to Time. Aelix had explained its power and how the aliens used it to stay ahead of humanity, predicting every move the resistance made. If there was any chance of reversing what had happened to her, of returning to her own time and seeing her family again, the Key was it.

But to get it, she had to enter the heart of the alien stronghold.

'I'm ready,' Ella whispered, her voice drifting in the wind like a promise.

Aelix stepped closer, their movements smooth, almost fluid. 'It's not just about the Key, you know. It's about all of this.' Aelix gestured to the crumbling city, the massive structures dominating the skyline like looming giants. 'Your people need hope.'

She swallowed hard, her fingers digging into her palms. 'I'm not their hope.'

'Maybe not yet,' Aelix said, their voice carrying the weight of centuries of knowledge. 'But once you cross that threshold, there's no going back.'

Ella didn't respond. She had spent too many sleepless nights replaying the same thoughts and doubts. What if she failed? What if this world was all that was left? What if her family and friends were gone, not just in time, but forever?

She couldn't let herself believe that. Not yet.

'When did your people arrive here, Aelix?' she asked.

'Forty years ago, as you measure time,' they replied.

So, ten years after she sank with the island and vanished.

'Were you part of the invasion?' she said.

They lowered their head. 'No. We have machines for that.'

Ella wanted to ask about Elementals, the Institute, and Earth's other defenders, but was afraid of the answers she might receive.

Maia approached from the shadows, glancing at Aelix. 'You sure you want to do this, Ella?'

'I'm your only hope of winning this war,' Aelix said.

Ella studied Maia's expression, knowing she didn't trust the alien, thinking it was all a ploy to infiltrate the resistance.

But what choice did she have?

What choice did humanity have?

They had to take Aelix back to the resistance and use their knowledge to create a clear plan to get inside the compound – no matter how risky that was.

But it was other people's lives Ella was risking now.

. . .

The underground bunker was dark and cramped, a series of narrow tunnels carved into the earth, hidden beneath the ruins of what had once been a shopping mall, and it buzzed with activity. People moved through the dim corridors, their faces grim but determined. There were whispers whenever someone saw Aelix, startled expressions, and the occasional gasp. Maia had searched the alien before they'd left the cliffs, removing Aelix's clothes and giving them a shirt and trousers from Maia's bag. It was as thorough as they could get, but Ella understood a tracking device might be inside Aelix.

She followed Aelix through the maze of tunnels, her nerves fraying with every step. The deeper they went, the more isolated she felt. This wasn't her world. These weren't her people. And she was putting them all at risk.

They reached a vast chamber where a group of resistance fighters had gathered around a makeshift table. Maps and blueprints were spread across the surface, illuminated by a single hanging light. Hard-faced men and women scrutinised the alien in their midst, and Ella assumed most wanted to jump up and strangle Aelix. Maia had radioed ahead to warn them what she was bringing back, but they still seemed shocked by their new ally.

She stood on the outskirts, watching. There was a rawness in the atmosphere, a desperation that clung to them like a second skin. Many looked scarred, worn down from years of fighting, their faces hard from the weight of survival. They moved with purpose, but their eyes had an underlying exhaustion. They were fighters, but they were also human—humans who had lost homes, families, friends —just like her.

Maia spoke like a leader. 'We'll only have one opportunity at this. We move in small teams, each with specific targets. Our goal is the Key, but the aliens won't make it easy. We strike hard, and we hit them fast. Our target is the floating fortress here.' She pointed to a spot on the map, an access point – according to Aelix – leading into the compound above. 'That's where they're keeping the Key. We might have a chance if we can get in and out without raising alarms.'

"Might'?' one of the fighters muttered, crossing his arms. 'That's not reassuring.'

Maia glared at him. 'This is the best shot we've got. The Key is our only hope to turn the tide. If we can get it, we can fight back.'

The room fell silent, the significance of her words settling over the group. Ella felt a knot form in her stomach. This was real. This wasn't just some vague plan or distant goal. They were going to do this.

'How do we get off the ground and into the floating compound?' a man asked.

'There's a chute that leads upwards. We'll take that,' Maia replied.

'Where did you get these details?' a woman said, even though everybody knew the answer.

Doctor Santos spoke up. 'Aelix is not the first alien to help the resistance.' Gasps went around the room. 'It's not information we share with everyone.' He glanced at Aelix. 'But I believe we can trust them.'

Aelix stepped forward. 'The Key is heavily guarded. But I know where the security weaknesses are. I will get you inside.'

Maia and many others looked sceptical, but after a tense pause, she nodded. 'Fine. You lead us in, but the moment things go south, we abort. Understood?'

Aelix inclined their head. 'Understood.'

Maia's gaze shifted to Ella. 'You're with us now. No backing out. Once we're inside, we'll need all hands. You good with that?'

Ella met Maia's eyes, her heart hammering in her chest. 'I'm in.'

Maia nodded. 'Once we find this machine, we destroy it no matter what it takes? Right?'

Everyone else agreed, but Ella said nothing.

I have to use it first.

Aelix stood beside her. 'You don't have to do this alone.'

Ella peered at them. 'I know. But it doesn't make it any less terrifying.'

Aelix's voice softened. 'Courage isn't the absence of fear. It's pushing forward despite it.'

Ella let out a shaky breath, nodding. Fear was a constant companion, gnawing at the edges of her mind, but it didn't have to stop her.

The hours passed in a blur of preparation. Weapons were distributed, maps memorised, and final instructions given. The resistance fighters moved efficiently, each task honed by years of necessity. Ella watched them, her nerves a live wire beneath her skin. She had never held a weapon like the one they gave her—a sleek, alien blaster that felt heavy and foreign.

Aelix, noticing her discomfort, approached. 'It's not about strength. It's about precision. You don't have to be the best shot. Just stay calm.'

'Calm,' she repeated, a bitter smile tugging at her lips. 'Easier said than done.'

Aelix's eyes gleamed in the gloom. 'It always is. But you're here. That's what matters.'

She glanced at the blaster, her fingers tracing the unfamiliar curves of the weapon. Her mind wandered to her parents—her mother's laugh, her father's steady voice, the warmth of their presence. It felt like a lifetime ago, like another person's memories. Would they even recognise her now? Would she?

'Ella.' Aelix's voice pulled her back, gentle but firm. 'Focus.'

She blinked. 'Right. I'm ready.'

Aelix nodded, their eyes holding hers for a long moment before turning away. 'Good.'

The resistance set out when the sun dipped below the horizon. Silent as shadows, they slipped through the city's wreckage. The compound loomed in the distance, its jagged spires reaching into the sky like the claws of some great, terrible beast. Lights scanned the perimeter, and patrols of alien machines moved with rigid precision, their metallic forms gleaming under the harsh artificial lights.

Ella hunched behind a crumbling wall, her chest aching. Every instinct screamed at her to turn back, run, and hide. But she couldn't. She'd crossed the threshold when she agreed to the mission, and there was no escaping it.

Aelix crouched beside her, examining the compound. 'Stay close.'

Ella swallowed her fear. The others were in position, scattered across the perimeter, waiting for the signal to move. Maia's voice crackled in her earpiece. 'On my mark.'

The seconds stretched into what felt like hours, the tension suffocating. Ella's fingers tightened around the blaster, her pulse racing.

'Now,' Maia instructed.

They moved as one, slipping through the shadows and toward the compound. The air was thick with anticipation, every sound magnified in Ella's ears. The low hum of alien machinery, the distant clang of metal, and the soft thud of their footsteps against the ground created a symphony of impending danger.

As they neared the outer wall, Aelix signalled for them to stop. 'There,' they whispered, pointing to a narrow gap in the patrol patterns. 'We have thirty seconds. Move fast.'

Ella's heart leapt into her throat as she watched the machines march in perfect unison. Tension rippled through her, knowing one wrong move could mean the end for all of them.

'Go,' Aelix said.

They darted forward, slipping through the gap in the patrol as the machines moved out of range. Ella's breath came in shallow bursts as they reached the wall, pressing against the cold metal surface. She sensed the vibrations of the compound, a dim hum that seemed to pulse through her bones.

Maia motioned for them to move, leading the way as they crept along the wall, staying low to avoid detection. Ella's nerves frayed with every step. The structure loomed above them, a fortress of alien technology and power.

They crossed the threshold. There was no turning back.

Chapter 8

Reunion

The metallic hum of the compound vibrated through Ella's bones as she pressed against the cold wall of an abandoned building. The broken city was a maze of towering, strange spires, automated defences, and patrols. It stank of organic and mechanical decay, a fusion of human and alien remnants that churned her stomach.

Around her, the small group of resistance fighters moved like shadows, their footsteps silent, their expressions grim. They'd trained for this, hardened by years of hiding and surviving. But Ella felt the weight of inexperience. Each sound, every flicker of movement, made her heart race and her breath shallow.

'We'll have to cut through the central plaza,' Aelix whispered, their glowing eyes scanning the route ahead. 'The patrols are tight, but there's a gap every three minutes. We time it right, and we can slip through.'

Ella nodded, gripping her blaster tighter. The weapon felt strange in her hands, and the cold metal against her palms only heightened her unease. A distant whirring drew her attention. One of the alien drones—a sleek, black sphere hovering just above the ground—moved through the ruins, scanning the area with a faint blue light. She ducked lower, pressing herself against the wall.

'They're getting closer,' Maia whispered behind her.

'We wait,' Aelix said, never taking their eyes off the drone. 'Patience is key.'

Ella's pulse thundered in her ears as the drone floated past, its scanner sweeping over the ruins but missing them.

As the machine disappeared, Aelix nodded to the group. 'Time to move.'

They darted from their hiding place, slipping through the alleyways and shadows of the ruined city. The alien structures loomed above them, glowing with an eerie light. Ella's senses were heightened, sounds magnified, and every flicker of movement put her on guard. She'd never felt so exposed, so vulnerable.

The group paused as they reached the edge of the central plaza, a vast, open space that had once been a bustling square. Now, it was a barren wasteland, scarred by years of conflict. Alien machines moved in perfect synchronisation, their movements fluid and deliberate. Patrols of soldiers—alien and human collaborators—marched along the perimeter, their faces cold and expressionless.

Ella's stomach churned as she saw the humans working alongside the invaders. Collaborators. Traitors. She tightened her fingers around her weapon. It was hard enough fighting an alien force, but facing her own kind—people who had betrayed humanity for survival—felt like a different battle altogether.

They waited, watching the patrols with bated breath. The machines moved with clockwork precision, their glowing eyes scanning everywhere. The human collaborators followed in their wake, scanning for any signs of activity.

Aelix raised their hand, signalling the group to move. Ella's chest tightened as they slipped into the open plaza, sticking close to the shadows. The tension was unbearable, and every step could be their last. They moved quickly, silently, weaving through the debris and ruined structures.

Something caught her attention as they neared the plaza's centre - a man standing near an alien machine, talking to a group of collaborators. His back was to her, but he seemed familiar. Then he turned. She froze, struggling to breathe. Ginger hair. Tall, broad-shouldered. But what stood out most were his bright green eyes.

Ella recognised him.

No. It couldn't be.

He was older, much older than when she'd seen him last.

'Billy?' she whispered.

He didn't hear her, but she was unable to tear her gaze away. It looked just like him. Billy, her childhood friend. The boy who had been by her side through everything—the one she'd laughed with, fought with, dreamed with. But Billy had been fourteen when she last saw him, and that was... fifty years ago. This man was older, his face lined with age, but those eyes, that hair—she would recognise him anywhere.

She stepped forward before realising what she was doing, her mouth dry. 'Billy!'

Her voice echoed in the quiet night, and the alien machines froze. The collaborators turned, locking onto her, and in that moment, Ella knew she'd made a terrible mistake.

'Run!' Aelix yelled.

But it was too late. The machines whirred to life, their weapons glowing with a deadly light as they shifted toward Ella and the others. The collaborators shouted, drawing their guns.

Ella ducked behind a broken wall, her pulse pounding in her ears. 'Billy!' she shouted again, her voice raw with desperation. 'It's me! It's Ella!'

His eyes widened, a look of shock crossing his face. 'Ella? But you—'

There was no time for explanations. The machines were closing in, their weapons aimed at her. She fired her blaster, the bright beam cutting through the air, but the alien tech was faster. A barrage of lasers rained down on their position, forcing her to retreat.

Suddenly, the man—Billy—grabbed her arm, pulling her behind cover. 'Ella?'

She gazed at him, her mind in a whirlwind of activity. It was him. It was. But there was no opportunity to process the impossible.

'I can explain later,' she gasped. 'We have to move!'

Billy nodded, an expression of shock and confusion, but there was no time for questions. They sprinted through the ruins, weaving between the debris as the alien machines fired. The rest of the group scattered, Aelix shouting orders as they tried to regroup.

Ella's lungs burned, her ribs aching as they ducked behind an overturned vehicle.

'How are you here?' he asked, his voice breathless. 'You haven't aged a day.'

She shook her head, her mind spinning. 'I don't know. Something pulled me through time. It's complicated.'

'Complicated?' Billy gave her a look of disbelief. 'You

disappeared, Ella. Fifty years ago. We thought you were dead.'

'I'm not,' she said. 'But we have to focus. We need to get out of here.'

He peered at her as if she were a ghost. 'This isn't real. This can't be real.'

She glanced around, scanning for any sign of the others, but only saw Aelix. 'It's real, Billy. I don't know how or why, but I'm here now. And we have to find the Key.'

Billy frowned. 'The Key? You know about it?'

She nodded. 'The resistance, they think it's our only chance.'

Billy's expression darkened. 'That thing is dangerous, Ella. You don't realise what you're getting into.'

'I don't have a choice. It's the only way I can go back. The only way I can fix this.'

Billy stared at her for a long moment, his green eyes studying her. 'You haven't changed,' he whispered, almost to himself. 'Not even a little.'

She felt a lump in her throat, her chest tightening. She wanted to say so much and needed to explain, but there was no time. The alien machines were still searching for them, and they had to move.

'We'll talk later,' she said, forcing herself to focus. 'Right now, we need to survive.'

Billy's expression hardened. 'Follow me.'

They slipped through the shadows, moving deeper into the ruined city, with Aelix following in the shadows.

With Billy here, was this really her world?

Ella's mind churned as they moved, struggling to process the impossible reality before her. Billy was alive, but older by decades. He was supposed to be back in her time, in the life something had torn her from. Seeing him again felt like stepping into a warped dream that teetered between the comfort of familiarity and the sharp edge of betrayal. He'd been part of her past, yet there he was, entrenched in this dark, alien-dominated future.

'Keep low and stay quiet,' Billy whispered, glancing back at her with that same wary protectiveness she remembered from their childhood. His voice held the same familiar lilt, but it was deeper, roughened by years she hadn't witnessed. And he'd lost his accent.

They crept through the debris, ducking beneath twisted metal beams and sidling along crumbling walls. Ella caught glimpses of the alien compound looming above, casting an eerie glow over the city's ruins. The light bounced off the broken windows, and the metallic hum vibrated through her bones.

She wondered what had happened to Maia and the others, hoping they were safe. If they weren't, she would be to blame.

I ruined everything.

At least Aelix was there, close behind them. They slipped into a narrow alley hidden between two collapsed buildings. They crouched near a wall, the sound of distant patrols echoing around them. There was a second to breathe for the first time since the chaos erupted.

'Are you really here, Ella?' Billy's voice was soft, almost fearful.

She looked at him, seeing the worry in his expression, the decades etched into his face and felt a pang of guilt. 'I don't know how to explain it. One moment, I was sinking in the sea, and the next, I was here, fifty years later. For me, it's only been days, but for you—'

'Half a lifetime,' he finished.

'I'm sorry, Billy. I never wanted to leave. I don't even understand why I'm here.'

He shook his head, his expression softening. 'There's nothing to apologise for. But you've walked into a nightmare. The world's not what it was. It's twisted, darker.' He glanced at the alien structure looming in the distance. 'And it's all because of them.'

Ella followed his gaze, shuddering at the sight. 'The Key. Aelix said it's inside and lets them see and control the future. Is it true?'

Billy's jaw tightened, and a flicker of fear crossed his face. 'It's worse than that. The Key warps time itself. It's how they stay ahead, and it does something to people, something I can't explain. It's like they use the lives of humans to keep it running.'

Ella remembered Aelix's words about sacrifices and shivered. 'We must destroy it.'

Billy's gaze darkened. 'It's suicide, Ella. No one's ever made it inside, let alone close enough to touch the Key. The fortress is rigged with defences that sense movement, body heat, and intentions. If they think you're a threat, you're as good as dead.'

'I have to try,' she replied, her voice unwavering. 'I don't belong here, Billy. I have to find a way back to my time, and if there's a chance, even a small one, I'll take it.'

He shook his head. 'You don't understand, Ella. You're not just fighting soldiers or technology. That thing—the Key —is connected to them, to the invaders, in ways we can't comprehend. They would burn this entire city down to keep it out of reach.'

She peered at him, his face drawn with tension. He met her gaze, his eyes flashing with fear and determination. He was with her, risking everything, and for the first time, she felt the enormity of what this reunion truly meant. It wasn't just about them. It was about the world they shared, which she'd been pulled away from and was now fighting to return to.

Deep inside, she realised that finding Billy again was a sign.

Now Ella knew she was on the right path.

Chapter 9

Billy

'Stay here,' Billy said as he studied the area ahead.

The ruin of the city pressed in on all sides. Ella leaned against a crumbling wall. Her heart pounded in her ears, and she struggled to comprehend the last few minutes. The heat from the alien blaster still clung to her hands as her pulse thudded against the grip. She gazed at him, his broad shoulders rising and falling with the same laboured breaths.

Billy. The boy who used to climb trees with her, whose grin had once been so quick, so full of life. Now, there were no grins, no easy-going charm. There were only hard lines, deep-set wrinkles, and the haunted gaze of a man who had lived through hell.

'Billy,' she whispered again, still stunned. Her voice felt small in the hollowed-out building, drowned by the distant hum of the alien towers in the background.

'You know this traitor?' Aelix asked.

'Yes,' she replied. 'And he can't be a traitor.'

Aelix surveyed their surroundings. 'We're separated

from the others, but we can finish the plan. Is that what you want?'

She had no choice. And meeting Billy was a good omen, telling her she was on the right path.

'Billy?' she said.

He didn't answer. He wiped the sweat from his brow and glanced through the shattered window, scanning the streets like a soldier checking for patrols. He had a practised wariness about him, each movement deliberate, every breath measured. It was unnerving to see him like that. As a kid, he'd always been impulsive, running headlong into things.

'You disappeared fifty years ago,' Billy said, his voice low, eyes still on the street. 'We all thought you were dead when there were reports of that island sinking.'

Ella swallowed, the enormity of what he was saying crashing over her. 'I didn't die. I was transported. I don't even know how. One minute, I was fighting, and the next, I was drowning. And now I'm here.'

Billy gazed at her, his green eyes sharp, but there was a flicker of something softer beneath them, as if part of the boy he'd once been still recognised her. 'You don't look a day older.'

'I'm not,' she replied, shaking her head, trying to piece it together herself. 'I must have skipped forward. Fifty years. It was just a blink for me. But for you...' She trailed off, studying his face. Five decades had etched themselves into his skin, hardened his gaze. Her stomach twisted. 'What happened to you, Billy?'

He glanced away, jaw tight. 'That's a long story. And we don't have time for it. We must keep moving before those machines return.'

She wanted to push and ask a thousand more questions,

but Aelix interrupted before she could say anything else. 'Ella, we need to go.'

Ella's head snapped up, the urgency in Aelix's voice pulling her back into the present. The danger wasn't over. The machines were still out there, and the others were missing. Maybe they'd gone on ahead without them. They had a mission to complete.

But Billy...

'Are you a collaborator?' she asked him.

'No,' he replied, shaking his head. 'You don't understand, Ella. This isn't your fight.'

She blinked, stunned by the sudden coldness in his voice. 'Billy—'

'I'm not with the aliens,' he said, his eyes searching hers for understanding. 'I'm working undercover, but not with them.'

'What?' Ella's mind spun, trying to keep up with his words. 'You're... what do you mean?'

He sighed, the weight of years and secrets hanging on his shoulders. 'I'm working inside the alien structure, infiltrating it. But I'm not doing it for the resistance. I'm doing it for my family.'

Ella shivered. 'Your family?'

Billy nodded, the grim lines of his face deepening. 'We were living in one of the sectors – ghettos, really – when the aliens took them. My wife, my kids. They're holding them at one of their compounds. I've been cooperating. Pretending to work for the invaders. I'm trying to get my wife and kids out.'

She stared at him, disbelief mixing with a sharp sense of fear. 'You're working with the aliens?'

'Not by choice,' he said. 'You think I want to be doing this? They're keeping my family hostage, Ella. If I don't cooperate, they'll kill them. Or worse.'

The world felt too small, the air too thin. Ella's head hurt as she tried to comprehend the full scope of what Billy was saying. She hadn't even processed he was alive, let alone the idea he was working with the enemy. But she could see it in his face—he wasn't lying. The fear and pain were real, etched deep into his every expression.

'But why not go to the resistance?' she asked, her voice trembling. 'They could help you. We could help you.'

Billy shook his head again. 'No. The resistance can't help me, Ella. They lack the resources to break into the alien compound, and if they did, they'd never risk it for one family. They've got bigger priorities.'

She heard the bitterness in his voice, the anger building for years. 'So, you're doing this alone?'

'I don't have a choice.'

Billy had always been loyal and willing to fight for the people he cared about. Even when they were kids, he'd been the one to defend his friends and take the hit if it meant saving someone else. Now, that same loyalty was driving him to do something dangerous that could get him killed.

Ella's voice dropped to a whisper. 'What are you going to do, Billy?'

He hesitated for a moment. 'There's a mission coming up. A supply transport the aliens are sending to one of their research facilities. I will intercept it, slip inside the facility, and find my family.'

'That's suicide,' Ella said, her heart sinking. 'You can't do this alone.'

'I've been doing it alone for years,' he replied. 'I don't have another choice. I can't trust anyone with this.'

She moved towards him. 'You can trust me. Let me help

you. We can figure this out together. We can rescue your family.'

His eyes softened, and for the first time since they'd reunited, she saw a flicker of the old Billy—the boy who had once been her best friend. But then his gaze darkened again, and he shook his head.

'I can't ask you to do that. It's not like it was.' He gazed at her. 'After you left, there were no more sightings of Elementals or portals to other dimensions. The Institute left us alone with you gone. Do you still have the Book of All Life?'

'I lost it. Do you know what happened to my mum and dad?'

'No,' he replied. 'I never saw them again once you departed for the island.'

Ella's chest tightened at the mention of her old world, the memories of her parents and friends flooding back. But she pushed those thoughts aside. He was right—she had a mission. But that didn't mean she could walk away from him.

'You're my friend, Billy. I won't leave you to do this alone.'

He stared at her for a long moment, his jaw clenched tight. She recognised the conflict in his eyes—the need to protect her warring with the desperation to save his family.

'We'll figure it out,' he muttered. 'But not here. It's not safe.'

Ella agreed. She'd found Billy—against all odds, she'd found him. But now, she realised, the real challenge was only beginning.

Aelix's voice broke through the tension. 'We need to move.'

Billy turned to Aelix, as if seeing the alien for the first time. 'You're working with the humans?'

Aelix nodded. 'I am.'

An undercurrent of unease ran between them until Ella grabbed Billy's arm. 'What do you know about an Elemental Purge?'

Confusion rippled through his face. 'What?'

'A resistance commander mentioned it to me. Are you familiar with it?

He shook his head. 'No. After you left with your parents and Seraphina, I stayed home with Hannah and waited for you to return. But we heard nothing apart from the island sinking in the North Sea.'

Hannah. Ella had forgotten about Billy's cousin.

'Where's Hannah?' she asked.

He sighed. 'She vanished years ago when the aliens invaded. Lots of people did.' He turned toward the exit, peeking out to check the streets. 'Come on. I know a place where we can lie low. It's not far.'

She followed him, her mind whirling. She couldn't believe what he'd been through. What he was still going through. But one thing was clear: this world had broken him, twisted him into someone she barely recognised.

Now, she was determined to help him, no matter what.

Chapter 10

Revelation

They crept through the ruined streets, shadows slipping between broken walls and piles of debris. Every step echoed the heavy weight of fifty years that had stretched between them, a gap filled with questions, regrets, and the alien war that had reshaped the world.

Billy led them, checking their surroundings, someone accustomed to surviving in the harshest conditions. His steps were sure, his movements efficient, even though his face betrayed the strain of years spent fighting battles Ella couldn't imagine.

She followed close behind, her gaze fixed on the man she'd once called a friend. There was an invisible barrier between them—a lifetime lived apart. Aelix brought up the rear, his alien senses tuned to dangers neither of them could perceive, his agenda still a mystery even as he appeared to aid her.

'Just up here,' Billy said, nodding towards a narrow alley between two crumbling buildings. His voice sounded strained, a roughness that hadn't been there before—the weight of five decades.

Ella kept pace with him, her eyes darting between shadows. The alien structures loomed in the distance, their silver spires reflecting the cold light of the cloudy sky. After several turns and passages, he led them through the shattered doorway of what had once been a pub. The sign above it, faded and barely legible, read The Red Lion, though the lion's face had long since worn away. Inside, it was dark, and the smell of damp and decay clung to her.

'We'll be safe here for a bit,' he muttered, crouching low, listening for any signs of pursuit. When he was satisfied, he turned to them.

'You've done this before,' Aelix remarked.

Billy grimaced. 'More times than I care to count.'

She recognised the exhaustion etched into his face, the way his shoulders sagged, as though the fight had drained every ounce of life from him, leaving only a shell behind. But there was still something there, some spark of the boy he used to be, buried deep beneath the decades of struggle. It made her heart ache to see him like that.

'I never thought I'd meet you again,' Ella said. She was lost, unsure where to start, how to make sense of everything. Part of her still couldn't believe it—fifty years had passed, and Billy, her best friend, had lived through all of them.

'Neither did I,' he replied. He sank into a chair, his head resting in his hands, before looking at her again. 'After you disappeared... everything changed. The world fell apart.'

She swallowed hard. 'Tell me.'

He hesitated, glancing at Aelix. 'Is the alien your friend?'

Ella nodded. 'Aelix is helping us – helping me.'

'Okay,' Billy began, leaning back in his chair as if

remembering was painful. 'It was years after you vanished. At first, we thought the Institute was involved. I was convinced they'd taken you. But then the invaders arrived.'

Ella's heart tightened.

'It was sudden,' he continued, his eyes dark, distant. 'Nobody saw it coming. One day, everything was normal, and the next, the sky was full of their ships. Huge, hulking things, like something out of a nightmare. They tore through our defences like paper. Nothing could stop them.'

Ella listened in silence.

'They came in waves,' he said. 'At first, they just destroyed everything—cities, military bases, anything that could be used to fight back. People tried to resist, but it was no use. Their technology was... it's beyond anything we've ever seen. They can manipulate energy and control machines with their minds. We never stood a chance.'

He rubbed a hand over his face, the weight of the years evident in each line, every scar. 'After the first few months, they started rounding people up. Anyone who survived the initial attacks was killed or taken to labour camps. They divided places into sectors and created a rationing system where people needed ID cards for food and resources, housing and supplies. Then they built those...' He gestured in the direction of the towering alien structures outside. 'We don't know what they're doing inside them, but it can't be good.'

Ella's stomach twisted. She'd seen those towers—tall, gleaming things that pulsed with a strange energy. She'd felt their presence in the air, how they hummed with power.

'Why didn't the Elementals do anything?' she asked. 'How come nobody fought back?'

Billy's expression hardened. 'The Elementals vanished after you did. There were no more portals, no more sightings of them. Some people said they'd abandoned us. Others thought they'd been destroyed. But whatever took place, they weren't there when we needed them.'

Ella felt a sharp pang of guilt at his words. She hadn't meant to abandon anyone. Now, hearing the devastation that had followed her disappearance, she couldn't help but wonder if there was something she could have done. Could she have made a difference if she hadn't been on that island when it sank into the sea?

'What happened to you on that island, Ella?'

She glanced at Aelix, considering how much to reveal and if she should trust him.

'Do you remember Seraphina?' she said.

Billy nodded. 'How could I forget the witch? Did she betray you?'

She shook her head. 'No, quite the opposite. She used her dragon to take me, my parents, and a few others to the North Sea island. There, we met other Elementals Seraphina had rescued from the Institute. She used her Light – her magic – to keep the island hidden from the world while we considered what to do next. But there was a bigger problem on the island.'

He shivered. 'Pandora returned?'

'No,' Ella replied. 'As far as I know, she's still stuck in Everywhere. This problem was something else that had taken the power of Pandora, Elementals, and all of humanity to defeat hundreds of thousands of years before – The Soulless.'

'The Soulless?' Billy asked.

'An ancient creature bent on consuming our world. We were fighting it when the Institute invaded the island, and everything went to hell.' She sighed. 'And I woke up here.'

'Shit!' Billy said.

'Fascinating,' Aelix added.

Ella faced the alien. 'Does any of that mean something to you?'

'What are Elementals?' Aelix asked.

Ella flexed her fingers, feeling pain ripple through her hands. 'Living things that we – humans – thought were only myths, legends, and superstitions. But we were wrong.'

'And you fought against them?' Aelix said.

'Some were friends, others were enemies,' Ella replied.

Aelix considered her words. 'And they lived in other realms, other dimensions, to this one?'

'Yes,' she answered. 'They travelled here through portals. If some of those still exist, I might be able to get Elementals to help us against the invaders.'

'Fascinating,' Aelix repeated. 'When we first arrived on this planet, our scientists discovered several remnants of energy fields they theorised may have been used to travel between worlds.'

Ella's heart raced. 'Remnants?'

'Yes,' Aelix said. 'Energy doorways, I suppose, but someone – or something – had destroyed them all.'

Ella slumped against the wall. 'The Elemental Purge.'

'What?' Billy asked.

The room spun before her, and she had to take a deep breath to calm her nerves. 'That must have been what Chen meant. The Institute, or world governments, blew up all the portals and killed all the Elementals they'd imprisoned.'

'Shit!' Billy shouted. 'And this was after what happened to you and the others on the island?'

Ella wanted to bang her head against the wall. 'I guess so. Many people died there even before it sank.' She stared at him. 'If that hadn't happened, there would have been

Elementals around who could have helped humanity fight the aliens when they arrived.'

Billy's voice softened. 'We tried, Ella. People resisted and did what they could, but it was hopeless.'

'And you've been fighting ever since,' she whispered, her heart aching for him while her guilt threatened to over-whelm her.

Billy nodded. 'We've been trying to push back, but it's like battling a tidal wave. Every time we make progress, they wipe us out. Their machines are everywhere. They have eyes on everything.' He paused for a moment, focusing on Aelix again. 'And then there are the collaborators. Humans who've thrown in with the aliens for a chance at survival. They're the worst.'

'But not you?' Aelix said.

Billy glared at the alien. 'No. I told you. I only pretended to help *your* people to get to my wife and kids.'

'Help the invaders?' Aelix asked. 'How?'

Billy glanced at Ella. 'I did what I had to for my family, but I'm not a collaborator. They offer other humans as sacri-fices to the aliens.'

She shuddered at the thought. She'd always believed in the resilience of humanity, in the human ability to stand together in the face of adversity. But now, hearing about the collaborators, about the people who had turned against their own, she wasn't sure what to believe anymore.

'And your family?' Ella asked, knowing the answer from their earlier conversation, but needing to hear it again to make it real.

Billy's jaw tightened, and he looked away, his eyes fixed on a spot on the floor. 'They're inside one of the alien compounds. I've done everything possible to keep them safe. But I don't know how long I can keep this up.'

Ella's heart broke for him. She heard the desperation in his voice, the hopelessness from years of fighting a battle he couldn't win. And yet, despite everything, he'd kept going for his family.

'We'll get them out,' she said. 'We'll find a way, Billy.' She wouldn't let anyone down again.

He glanced at her, his green eyes full of doubt. 'You don't understand, Ella. This isn't something you can fix. It's not like the old days. The resistance doesn't have the resources to break into the alien strongholds. And even if they did, they'd never risk it for a few people.'

She tried to think of a plan, anything, that could help. But she didn't know enough about this world, the aliens, or their machines. She was out of her depth, and for the first time, she felt powerless.

Aelix spoke. 'The technology may seem insurmountable, but every system has flaws. Their power is not absolute.'

Billy scoffed, leaning back in his chair. 'Easy for you to say. You're one of them.'

'I was,' Aelix corrected, their voice cold. 'But I left for a reason. And that reason is standing near you.'

Billy frowned, glancing between Ella and Aelix. 'What are you talking about?'

Aelix's gaze shifted to Ella, their expression unreadable. 'The Key to Time. The device you've heard rumours about. It can do more than predict the future. It can reshape it.'

'Reshape the future?' Billy said. 'That's impossible.'

'Not for her,' Aelix replied, eyes locked on Ella. 'She can change everything. But she must understand what she is first.'

Ella's head spun, her thoughts crashing into each other as she tried to process Aelix's words. She'd always known she was different—her connection to the Elementals, her powers, her strange ability to survive where others hadn't. But to hear Aelix talk about her as if she was some saviour, some key to unlocking the future, unsettled her.

'I don't know what you're talking about,' she said, shaking her head. 'I'm just me.'

'No,' Aelix added. 'You're much more than that.'

Billy's gaze shifted to Ella, confusion and disbelief on his face. 'What does that mean?'

Ella looked at him, her heart heavy with the weight of everything she didn't understand. 'I don't know. But I think we're going to find out.'

Billy leaned forward, resting his elbows on his knees. His face was pale, his eyes haunted by the years of war, loss, and fear. Yet, despite all that, he looked at her with something she hadn't expected: hope. It was fragile, barely more than a flicker, but it was there.

'Then we better figure it out,' Billy said, his voice rough with exhaustion. 'Because right now, I've got nothing left to lose.'

Chapter 11

The Team

The rising sun cast pale, fractured light over the ruins, painting the city in shades of grey and amber. Ella's boots crunched against the cracked pavement as she followed Billy through the wreckage, her gaze lingering on the shadows stretching across the rubble. The city's silence was different in daylight—no less eerie but sharper, with a clarity that revealed each broken wall, each skeletal building stripped of life.

Billy moved with a silent efficiency, his focus razor-sharp. His hand rested on his weapon as he checked each alley and every crumbled facade as though he expected something to jump out at them from the desolation. There was no trace of the reckless boy she remembered—only a seasoned fighter who had learned the art of survival the hard way.

'Keep close,' he murmured. He didn't look back at her, and a distance in his tone gnawed at her, a reminder of the gulf of years and battles that separated them.

Ella kept her pace, with Aelix a few steps behind her, their alien eyes perusing the surroundings. Their presence was like a silent thread of tension—each movement deliberate, every step too light, too smooth, as though they were gliding rather than walking. Something was disquieting in Aelix's silence, in how they seemed to blend into the shadows, their expression unreadable.

They passed through an alley strewn with debris, the walls on either side charred and cracked, littered with remnants of old posters that flapped in the breeze. She glimpsed faded faces, messages of hope and resistance, yellowed and torn. Sorrow gripped her; they had belonged to a time when people believed they could still fight, that there was a way out. Now, even those symbols of defiance had been reduced to dust.

As they reached the end of the alley, Billy paused, raising a hand to signal them to stop. He turned, his expression grim. 'There's a checkpoint up ahead. The tunnels aren't far, but they've increased security around this part of the city.'

Ella's stomach tightened as she looked past him, seeing an alien patrol—a group of humanoid figures draped in armour, their faces hidden behind smooth, reflective helmets. They moved in eerie synchrony, their steps soundless, their weapons drawn and ready.

'What's the plan?' Aelix whispered.

Billy's gaze flickered to Aelix, a hint of distrust in his eyes. 'We wait for the shift change. There's a ten-minute gap between patrols. It's tight, but it's our only shot. Then we hit the tunnels and find the resistance.' He stared at Ella. 'Are you okay?'

She nodded. 'Sure.' She'd fought monsters, but not like these—not creatures that looked human but moved as if they were part of a single, unbroken mind. Every instinct screamed for her to run, but she forced herself to focus. 'Ten minutes. Got it.'

They crouched behind the wall, waiting as the patrol passed. Ella held her breath, feeling her heart beating, sensing each prickle of sweat on her skin. Billy remained fixed on the patrol, his face a mask of calm, though she recognised the tension in his clenched jaw. She wanted to talk to him about the life he'd lived, of what she'd missed, but fear gripped her – fear not born of the invaders nearby but of what she might discover about the boy she used to know.

Instead, she turned to Aelix, a thousand other questions buzzing inside her head. She started with one. 'Do you miss your home planet?'

Aelix's eyes shimmered like a universe of endless, glistening stars. 'Thelxon? No. There's nothing for me there.'

Aelix's face softened as they looked back toward the shadowed alleyway, their gaze distant, as though they could see past this devastated world's ruins and fractured buildings. Their eyes sparkled, their depths revealing something Ella hadn't noticed before—a sadness that seemed to stretch far beyond the boundaries of this battle, beyond even this world.

'Aelix,' she asked, 'what did you leave behind?'

For a moment, Aelix was silent, their face unreadable. Then, as if something deep within them had given way, they spoke, a voice low and almost detached, like they were reciting someone else's story.

'My family,' Aelix said, the words hanging heavy between them. 'On Thelxon, loyalty is conditional, but we still have bonds. I had a sister. Aya.' They paused, fingers shaking. 'She was everything to me.'

Ella held her breath, listening as they continued, their voice carrying the weight of memories long buried.

'Aya differed from the others. She questioned things. Asked why the Thelxons never considered compassion, why we only took and conquered. She believed we could be more than what we are.' Aelix's expression tightened, and a flicker of pain crossed their face. 'I thought I could protect her. But when she grew older, they learned about her questions and ideas. They separated her from me.'

Ella's heart twisted, empathy slicing through her anger and suspicion. She pictured a younger version of Aelix, determined and hopeful, trying to hold on to a family that a cruel world kept tearing from them.

'Did you ever track her down?' she asked, though she could already sense the answer.

Aelix's gaze dropped to the ground. 'No. I left Thelxon in search of her. But I knew before I started looking that I wouldn't find her. The Thelxons don't tolerate those who challenge their ways.' Their voice turned cold, each word bitter and edged with regret. 'Aya is gone, and my people are strangers to me now – enemies, even.'

Ella's body tensed. She understood loss, but Aelix's was of a different kind—they hadn't just lost someone; they'd lost an entire world, as she had. She moved closer, her voice soft. 'I'm sorry, Aelix. I didn't know.'

A ghost of a smile touched Aelix's lips. 'I wouldn't expect you to. But maybe that's why I stayed—why I chose to fight alongside you, even though I could have left.'

'Because of Aya?'

Aelix nodded. 'I saw something of her in you—in your defiance, your unwillingness to surrender. Even when you're terrified, you keep fighting. She was like that. She believed that one day, people like us might change the fate of countless worlds.'

Ella's heart ached for the loss Aelix carried, a burden they kept to themselves until now. She hesitated before touching Aelix's arm. 'You're not alone in that. Whatever happens here, I'm with you.'

Aelix peered at her momentarily, something vulnerable breaking through their guarded expression. But just as quickly, the walls went back up, their gaze hardening.

A universe of silence settled between them.

Then, as the last soldier vanished down the street, Billy motioned for them to move. 'Now.'

They slipped from their hiding place, sticking to the shadows as they rushed toward the entrance to the underground tunnels. Ella's senses were heightened, every sound amplified—the crunch of gravel beneath her boots, the distant hum of machinery, the faint rustling of debris in the breeze. She sensed Aelix's presence at her back, their movements as smooth and soundless as a wraith's.

They reached the entrance, a rusted metal door half-buried in rubble. Billy knelt, clearing away a few stones before he pulled it open, revealing a dark stairwell descending into the earth. The stench of damp stone and mildew wafted up, mingling with the metallic taste of rust and rot. The air was thick and suffocating, as though the city's decay had seeped into every crack and crevice.

'After you,' Billy muttered, gesturing for Ella to go first.

Ella swallowed, peering into the darkness before stepping onto the narrow staircase. The steps groaned beneath her, and she gripped the cold metal railing, her knuckles white. She descended, her heart hammering with each step, the shadows closing around her. The walls felt close, pressing in from all sides as if the ruin above was ready to bury them alive.

Aelix followed, and she heard Billy as he brought up the rear. The silence in the stairwell was dense and oppressive, broken only by the drip of water echoing from somewhere below. She couldn't shake the feeling of descending into a tomb.

They reached the bottom, where a narrow passage stretched before them, lit by a flickering light mounted to the ceiling. The walls were rough, carved from stone and reinforced with rusted metal beams, the scent of decay lingering everywhere.

Billy moved past her, leading the way down the corridor. His face was set, his gaze fixed straight ahead, but Ella glimpsed something haunted in his eyes, a shadow that lingered just beneath the surface.

They reached a small room off the side, cluttered with makeshift supplies—a few rations, tools, and a stack of faded maps. Graffiti lined the walls; messages scrawled in haste, some in languages Ella didn't recognise. She touched one message, feeling the roughness of the paint beneath her skin.

'They come here sometimes,' Billy said. 'Refugees from the city. They hide, rest, and then move on. Few of them stay long. Nobody does.'

Ella turned to him. 'It's hard to believe this is what's left. All those people we knew, all those places gone.'

His expression softened. 'It's not the world you remember, Ella. Everything's changed now. People are different. They've had to be.'

She studied his face, noting the lines etched into his skin and the hard glint in his eyes. 'And you?'

He held her gaze for a long moment, his jaw tight. 'I've done things I'm not proud of. Things I had to do to survive, to keep my family safe.'

Aelix stepped forward, breaking the tension. 'Survival has cost us all. It's a cruel reality, but it keeps us alive.'

Billy's focus flickered to Aelix. 'It's easy to say that when you're outside, watching. It's a different story when you're in the thick of it.'

Aelix's expression didn't change, but there was a glimmer of something dark in their eyes. 'Believe me, I know the cost of survival all too well. I've seen more suffering than you can imagine. I may not be human, but I understand pain.'

Billy's jaw clenched, but he didn't respond. Instead, he turned away, examining the maps spread across a makeshift table in the corner. Ella sensed the tension between them, the distrust simmering beneath the surface. He looked at Ella. 'Will you lead the way?'

She nodded. 'Follow me.'

Ella moved through a narrow tunnel, slipping on the night vision glasses Maia had given her when they'd set off on the original mission to the alien compound. She didn't look back, hearing the others behind her. She thought of Maia again, hoping her new friend had survived and returned to the resistance.

How many people died because of my stupid mistake?

After a tense journey, they reached the entrance to the headquarters—a hidden steel entrance embedded in the side of a collapsed skyscraper. Billy knocked in a pattern Ella didn't recognise, and the door creaked open.

Inside, the rebel base buzzed with activity. Makeshift equipment, resistance fighters, and the constant hum of radio chatter filled the underground warren of rooms and tunnels. Maia stood waiting for them, her arms crossed, studying them as they entered. Her gaze lingered on Billy, her expression unreadable.

Ella wanted to run to Maia, to throw her arms around her in relief. But she didn't.

'Ella,' Maia said, her voice steady but tinged with urgency. 'We need to talk.'

Ella nodded, glancing at Billy before following Maia into a side room. Aelix and Billy stayed behind, though she sensed their eyes on her as she walked away.

Maia closed the door and turned to face her.

'What happened out there? Who is he?'

Ella took a deep breath, trying to gather her thoughts. 'His name is Billy. He was my best friend before. Before I disappeared. He survived the invasion, but he's been working undercover inside the alien structure.'

Maia's expression darkened. 'Inside the alien structure? And he just showed up now?'

'He's not working with the aliens,' Ella said. 'They're holding his family hostage. He's trying to save them.'

Maia narrowed her eyes, her suspicion clear. 'And you trust him?'

Ella hesitated. 'I do. I've known Billy my whole life. He's not a collaborator. He's just stuck.'

Maia studied her for a long moment before sighing. 'We've been betrayed before, Ella.'

Ella nodded. 'Did anyone get hurt?'

'What, when you alerted the aliens to our presence?'

Ella's hand trembled, a knot forming in her heart. 'I'm sorry.'

She was about to ask again when there was a knock at

the door, and Aelix stepped inside. 'We have little time,' they announced, their voice cold and precise. 'The alien forces are increasing their patrols. They'll find this place soon enough.'

Maia glanced at Aelix, her eyes narrowing. 'Why are you different from those that have enslaved us?'

'I gave you my reasons,' Aelix answered.

'You call them aliens, but they're your people.'

'The collaborator humans – are they your people?' Aelix asked.

She shook her head. 'You've got inside knowledge of the aliens' movements. That makes you valuable—but also dangerous.'

They met her gaze, unflinching. 'I understand your concerns, but stopping the invaders will take more than resistance fighters with guns. You require a strategy, and you'll need to know their weaknesses. After last night's events, they'll have increased their security. We'll have to come up with another way to get inside.'

Maia leaned against the wall, considering his words. 'All right. Let's hear it.'

Aelix's gaze shifted to Ella. 'Ella is strategic to stopping them. She has the potential to unlock the power of the Key and disrupt their control.'

'Why her?' Maia asked.

Ella held her breath.

'Ella fell through time,' Aelix said. 'I should have realised it sooner, but that wasn't a coincidence. There must be a connection between her and the Key to Time.'

'Why her?' Maia asked again.

Aelix shrugged. 'I don't know.'

Maia was silent for a long moment before nodding.

'Okay. But we lost some good people last time.' More guilt swept through Ella. 'We'll need a new team.'

'I know folks,' Billy declared from the doorway. 'There are fighters who can help. But it won't be easy.'

Maia's expression hardened. 'It never is. Let's get started.'

Over the next few hours, Maia and Aelix worked together to devise a new plan. Ella watched as they pored over maps and schematics of the alien fortress to find the best way in, something different from what they'd planned before.

Before I ruined everything when I saw Billy.

She met those who would play a crucial role in the new mission. The first was Erin. She was tall, with a muscular build and sharp, intense eyes that missed nothing. Her hair was cropped short, and her face was lined with the scars of a dozen battles. She radiated strength and determination, but there was wariness in her gaze when she looked at Ella.

'So, you're the girl who appeared out of nowhere,' Erin said, her tone blunt as she sized Ella up. 'Heard a lot of stories about you.'

Ella shifted under the scrutiny. 'Not all of them are true.'

Erin snorted. 'I'll believe it when I see it. We've had enough 'saviours' over the years who turned out to be nothing more than fairy tales.'

Ella nodded, understanding her scepticism. 'I'm not here to be a saviour. I want to help.'

Erin studied her for another moment before nodding. 'Good. We don't crave heroes. We need people who can get the job done.'

Next, Billy introduced her to Jay, a teenage hacker. He was thin, with messy hair and a mischievous smirk that seemed out of place in their grim world. But despite his light-hearted demeanour, his eyes showed sharp intelligence.

'You're the tech expert?' Ella asked as Jay tinkered with a small device, his fingers moving over the wires.

'Expert? Nah,' he said with a grin. 'More like a guy who likes to mess with things until they work. But yeah, I'm your man if you need to hack into alien systems or disable a security grid.'

Ella smiled at his enthusiasm. 'Good to know.'

Jay winked. 'Just point me in the right direction.'

Finally, there was Zara, who worked inside the fortress, taking food to prisoners before they were transported elsewhere. Billy knew her from his undercover work. She was striking, with dark hair that fell in loose waves around her shoulders and eyes that seemed to see through you. There was an air of secrecy about her, a quiet confidence that made it clear she was used to navigating dangerous situations.

'You're the spy?' Ella asked, her voice low as she studied Zara.

Zara smiled. 'That's what they call me. I prefer to think of myself as adaptable.'

Ella raised an eyebrow. 'Adaptable enough to infiltrate the alien stronghold?'

Zara's smile widened, though there was something dangerous in her expression. 'I have my ways. And if you want to get close to the Key to Time, you'll need someone who can move between worlds without being noticed.'

With the team assembled, the plan took shape. They would penetrate the structure during the transport of supplies, using Aelix's inside knowledge of alien operations and Jay's hacking skills to turn off security measures. Zara would provide access to critical points within the structure, while Erin would provide the firepower to fight their way through when needed.

Ella studied them all as they prepared, but all she could think of was the others who had already died in this terrible future because of her.

Chapter 12

The Plan

The faint light from the hanging bulbs flickered like deranged fireflies, creating long, uneven shadows on the crumbling walls. Anticipation and fear filled the air, with the quiet buzz of machines and the distant murmurs of resistance fighters providing the only noise. The weight of the world seemed to rest on Ella's shoulders with each step she took. Her boots dragged on the floor, her mind wandering while her body felt restless.

She stopped outside the main war room. The voices inside, low and urgent, tugged at her consciousness, drawing her back to the present. For a moment, she leaned against the wall, closing her eyes, taking in the sounds: the faint clatter of weapons being prepped, the hushed conversations between fighters planning their next move, the distant mechanical buzz of Jay tinkering with another of his hacked devices.

But it was the quiet voice in her head, her voice, that she couldn't shake.

The Key to Time. Could I really do it? Could I change the past? And if I do, what happens to all of these people?

She felt the pull deep in her gut, a tight knot of longing and fear. The possibility was there, right in front of her, so close. Aelix had made it clear—the Key had the potential to disrupt the aliens' control, yes, but it could do more. It could manipulate time itself. That implied she could go back, no matter how slight the chance. Undo everything. Save her parents and her friends. Maybe even stop the invasion before it started.

But the thought came with an icy whisper of danger. She knew the consequences could be disastrous. The threads of time weren't meant to be unravelled without tearing apart reality. Was she prepared to risk that? Was she willing to gamble the future for the chance to rewrite the past?

And what price would be paid?

A voice snapped her out of her thoughts.

'Ella?'

She blinked and turned. It was Billy. He stood a few feet away, hands in his pockets, a tense look on his face. His shoulders were hunched, his whole posture tight as though he'd been carrying a heavy burden for too long.

'Hey,' she said.

'You okay?' His tone was casual, but his eyes had an undercurrent of worry. He stepped closer, studying her as if he could read her thoughts by looking at her.

Ella forced a smile. 'Yeah, I'm fine. Just thinking.'

Billy nodded, but he didn't press. They stood in silence for a moment, the noise of the base muffled around them. His presence was comforting, in a way, familiar, even though so much had changed between them. He was still Billy, the boy she'd known all her life, but he had a hardness now, a sharp edge that hadn't been there before.

He reached into his jacket and removed a small wallet.

He opened it to show her a photo of a smiling woman and two teenage girls who looked like twins. 'This is what I'm fighting for.'

She studied the picture. 'Your family?'

He nodded. 'Jessica and the girls – Hannah and Ella.'

She swallowed hard, trying to remove the lump in her throat. 'You named a daughter after me?'

Billy laughed. 'Of course – though the troublesome one is Hannah. I think she inherited my cousin's genes.'

They stood for a while before he put the wallet back.

'I was just talking with Zara,' he said after a long pause. 'She's confident she can get us close to the Key.'

Ella scrutinised him. His jaw was clenched, his eyes distant. There was something in his tone—something that made her stomach twist.

'Billy...,' she started, but the words caught in her throat.

He looked at her, and for a moment, the mask he'd been wearing slipped. She saw the fear in his expression, the desperation he tried so hard to hide. The same look he'd had earlier had been gnawing at her all day.

'I'm fine, Ella,' he said. His tone was tight and defensive. 'I can handle this.'

She took a step closer, lowering her voice. 'You're not fine. I see it. I'm worried about you.'

His jaw tightened, and for a second, she thought he would brush her off. But then his shoulders sagged, and he exhaled, running a hand through his messy hair.

'I don't have a choice,' he muttered. 'My family... they're still in there. Each day I wait, every second we delay, it's another day they could—' His voice cracked, and he looked away, his hands balling into fists at his sides.

Ella felt a lump rise in her throat. She reached out, touching his arm. 'I understand.'

His eyes flicked back to hers, a flicker of pain crossing his face. 'Do you?'

She hesitated and then nodded. 'I lost my family too, Billy. I don't even know if they're alive. But I understand what it's like to feel that kind of helplessness, to want to do something, anything, to change it.'

He was silent for a long moment, his gaze dropping to the floor. 'I just... I don't know how much longer I can keep going like this. Every time I close my eyes, I see them. I hear them calling out for me. And I'm powerless to do anything. I can't save them.'

His voice cracked, and Ella's heart ached for him. She tightened her grip on his arm. 'We'll get them out. We will. But we have to be smart about this. We could lose everything if you rush in there and make a mistake.'

He looked unconvinced. The tension in his body didn't ease, and Ella knew the words weren't enough. She sensed his desperation - like a living thing gnawing at him.

'I just... I can't lose them,' he whispered, almost to himself.

'You won't,' she said. 'Not if we do this together.'

Billy straightened. 'Okay.' He smiled at her. 'Like old time's sake.'

The war room held a tension so thick that Ella thought she could see it shimmering in the air, like a fist ready to knock them all out. Maps, schematics, and hand-drawn diagrams of the alien fortress cluttered the large table in the centre. Maia stood at the head, her arms crossed over her chest, her sharp eyes flicking between the documents. Beside her, Aelix pointed to various points on the map, explaining the layout of the fortress and the security measures they'd need to bypass.

Ella and Billy slipped into the room, sitting near the

back. Erin, Zara, and Jay were already there, listening as Aelix spoke.

'There's a central hub here,' Aelix said, finger tracing a map route. 'It's where they control most of the internal security. If we can get Jay in there, he should be able to turn off the alarms long enough for us to move through the lower levels undetected.'

Jay grinned, leaning back in his chair. 'Piece of cake. I've cracked more complicated systems before breakfast.'

Ella admired his confidence, but it also worried her.

Erin, standing with her arms folded, gave him a sceptical look. 'You better hope you can, kid. Because if you screw this up, we'll all be dead before we get past the first checkpoint.'

Jay's grin faltered, but he recovered, shrugging. 'No pressure, right?'

Maia shot him a warning glance before returning to the map. 'The hidden passageway we found should bring us outside the fortress walls. From there, we move quickly. The patrols are light in that area, but we can't afford to linger. Once we're inside, we'll split into teams. Jay, Aelix, and Zara will handle the security systems. Erin and her team will clear a path to the lower levels.'

'And what about us?' Billy asked, his voice cutting through the discussion.

Maia's gaze shifted to him. 'You and Ella are with me. Our job is to reach the Key. And we need to go up to do that.'

Ella shivered at the mention of the Key. She hadn't spoken to anyone about her fears or the thoughts that had haunted her since Aelix first mentioned its true power. The idea of controlling time and changing the past was too much. Too dangerous. But they needed it. Without the Key, they had no chance of stopping the aliens.

Or of her returning home.

'We'll have to move fast,' Aelix continued. 'The Key is well guarded. We'll only have a small window before they realise we're inside. If we fail—'

'We won't,' Billy cut in, his voice hard.

Aelix glanced at him. 'Let's hope you're right.'

There was a brief silence as everyone processed the gravity of the situation. Maia cleared her throat, drawing everyone's attention back to her. 'Get some rest. We leave at dawn. Be ready.'

The meeting broke up, and the group dispersed to their tasks. Ella lingered near the table, her eyes scanning the maps before her. Billy stood beside her, his presence a steadying force even as her mind raced with a hundred different thoughts.

'You okay?' he asked.

She hesitated, then nodded. 'Yeah. Just a lot to take in.'

'You don't have any doubts?' he said.

A million, but I can't tell you or the others.

'No. You?'

He shrugged. 'It's probably a suicide mission, but none of this would be possible without your alien friend.'

'You still don't trust Aelix?'

'Do you?'

'I have to,' she answered. 'I won't get home otherwise.'

He nodded. 'Remind me how you met them again.'

Ella sighed. She'd told the story dozens of times to him and everyone else who had asked her. But she repeated it anyway. 'Satisfied?'

He shook his head. 'It's a hell of a coincidence they bumped into you when they did, don't you think?'

'How many aliens have you spoken to, Billy?'

He grimaced. 'You believe I'm a traitor, a collaborator?'

She grabbed his hand. 'No, of course not. You're my old friend, Billy Pudding, the kid who stood by my side as we fought harpies and dragons and witches.'

'And Pandora?' he added.

Ella smiled, remembering a lifetime ago, though it was only two years to her. 'Yeah, and Dora.' She gripped his fingers. 'And the Institute. They all seemed stronger than us, but we survived. And we'll survive this. I only asked about your dealings with the aliens because I'm curious if you noticed anything strange about talking to them.'

His laugh warmed her hand. 'Everything about them is strange, Ella.'

She touched her neck. 'What about that unusual symbol they all have? Do they use that to communicate between them?'

'Maybe, I'm unsure. Why?'

'When you spoke with any of them,' she said. 'Did the symbol move?'

He thought for a second. 'No, I don't think so. Why?'

She pulled him closer and lowered her voice. 'Because it moves slightly when they're near me. I suspect it could have something to do with Light.'

His eyes widened. 'Do you still have Light inside you?'

She shook her head. 'I don't think so. There may be a tiny recollection of it there, like a ghost, but I find nothing every time I search inside myself for it.'

Billy rubbed his chin. 'But you think there might be a connection between what's left in you and that alien symbol they all have on their necks?'

She frowned. 'Yes, I do. And it worries me.'

He touched her shoulder. 'We're going to get through this. We have to.'

She glanced up at him, offering a small smile. 'Yeah. We do.'

But as he walked away, Ella couldn't shake the unease in her chest. She turned back to the map, her eyes drawn to the section marked 'Key to Time.' It was circled in red, the lines leading to it like a labyrinth of danger.

If I use it, what will happen?

She could change everything. Rewrite history. Save her family. But the consequences might be catastrophic. Time wasn't meant to be controlled like that. And yet, the temptation was there, lurking just beneath the surface, whispering to her.

Ella pushed the thoughts aside. There was no time for hesitation. The mission was all that mattered.

The hours ticked by, the tension in the base growing thicker as the moment for departure neared. She wandered through the dark corridors, her mind too restless for sleep. She passed the armoury, where Erin's team was prepping their weapons, the cold gleam of metal catching the light. Jay was crouched in a corner, muttering to himself as he adjusted the wiring on one of his devices, his fingers moving with practised precision.

Everybody appeared focused, preparing for what was to come—everyone except her.

She stood before a cracked mirror, its surface clouded with dust. Her shattered reflection stared back at her, the dark circles under her eyes a testament to the sleepless nights and endless battles. She barely recognised herself anymore. The girl she'd once been, the one who had laughed with her friends and spent summer days lying in the grass, dreaming about the future—that girl was gone. In her place was a warrior, hardened by loss and pain, driven by a need for revenge. But beneath that armour, the fear was still there. The doubt. The uncertainty about what lay ahead.

Ella reached up, brushing a strand of hair behind her ear as she studied her reflection. She could almost hear her younger self whispering to her from the past.

Is this who you are now? Is this what you've become?

She closed her eyes, her hand dropping to her side.

What choice do I have?

There was no turning back. The Key was their only hope. If it could stop the aliens and end the war, she had to use it, even if it meant risking everything.

Even if it meant losing herself in the process.

Dawn came too quickly. The base was alive with movement as the resistance fighters gathered in the main chamber, their expressions grim and focused. Ella stood with the others, her pack slung over her shoulder, her heart pounding. The hidden passageway awaited them, a dark tunnel leading to the unknown.

Maia was at the front, her voice steady as she gave the final briefing. 'Remember the plan. Stick to your teams. We move fast, and we stay quiet. Once we're inside, we don't stop. No hesitation.' Her eyes swept over the group, landing on Ella before moving on. 'And no stupid mistakes.'

Ella tightened her grip on her weapon, feeling its weight in her hands. Beside her, Billy adjusted the strap on his pack. He glanced at her, offering a slight nod.

'You ready?' he asked.

She nodded, though her stomach churned with nerves. 'Yeah.'

They left in silence. The passageway, dark and foreboding, the walls slick with moisture, loomed ahead. She shivered as they descended into the tunnel, the air growing colder with each step. The darkness surrounded them, the narrow corridor just wide enough to move in single file. The only sound was the soft shuffling of their footsteps, the occasional drip of water echoing through the stone.

Ella's thoughts spiralled as they moved deeper into the tunnel. The Key was waiting for them somewhere in the heart of the alien fortress. And with it, the power to change everything. But as they approached their goal, Ella couldn't shake the feeling that something was watching them.

Chapter 13

The Journey

The narrow passage stretched endlessly, the walls pressing in as they moved deeper beneath the ruined city. Ella's pulse vibrated in her ears, her senses alive to every sound—the quiet shuffle of boots on slick stone, the drip of water somewhere in the darkness. It felt like they were descending into the belly of some ancient, slumbering beast, and each step brought them closer to its heart.

She remembered a time, as a kid, exploring London's abandoned underground. The memory came rushing back, vivid and unbidden, filling the silence around her as they crept through the passage. It had been a foggy November afternoon, damp and grey. Ella had been only ten back then, fearless in that way kids could be, always hungry for an adventure. The derelict station had beckoned to her, hidden behind rusted gates and crumbling walls, a forgotten world beneath the bustling city. Her parents had warned her, but curiosity had won out.

She'd ducked through a narrow gap in the fence, slipping past peeling posters advertising decades-old shows and snacks, and found herself in the tunnel's mouth. It stank of ancient, stale air and damp metal, the silence pressing down like a secret. Her footsteps echoed off the stone as she walked deeper, the daylight fading behind her.

In those moments, her breath quickening with each step, she'd felt the thrill of discovery—of uncharted territory and forbidden places. Her imagination had spun tales of forgotten trains, ghostly passengers, and hidden passageways to realms unknown.

Ella had wandered for hours, the silence broken only by her footsteps and the occasional drip of water, reaching the end of the tunnel, where the darkness appeared endless like a gaping maw waiting to swallow her whole. The faint chill of fear crept into her. The walls had seemed closer, the air denser, as if something ancient and forgotten lay just beyond the shadows. Then she saw an old control room with the messages scratched into the walls.

The images flashed before her: the faded console covered in dust, the switches frozen in time. But it was the messages that had haunted her—the scratches, the desperate etchings from those trapped there during the bombings, waiting for help that never came. She'd traced her fingers over the jagged letters, their pleas and farewells, their fear etched into the stone for eternity.

I'm still here.

Ella had tried to understand it, wanting to know what it felt like—to be waiting there, to know no one was coming. In the silence that followed, she felt the weight of that forgotten fear pressing in, mingling with the terror of the present, of the ruins above and the secrets hidden within them. She'd stood in that control room, feeling like the shadows would close around her, that she might become part of those etched words.

Ella focused on the now, clenching her fists to steady her breathing. She sensed Billy's eyes on her, his presence a silent, grounding force. But the memory, that old fear of being trapped in the darkness, lingered, pressing at the edges of her mind.

Maia led the way, her flashlight illuminating only a few feet ahead, casting an uneven, spectral glow on the jagged walls. The rest of the team moved in single file, tense and silent, their faces cast in shadow as they navigated the treacherous path. Ella felt the chill seeping through her clothes, her skin prickling with a cold that seemed to come not from the damp air but from the darkness, as if the earth held its own quiet malevolence.

Aelix walked close behind, their movements smooth and soundless, scrutinising every inch of their surroundings. Ella glanced back at them, searching for reassurance. Aelix's presence was both a comfort and a reminder of the alien fortress awaiting them—a place where Aelix claimed to have knowledge, but even that assurance felt tenuous.

Ahead of her, Billy moved with the ease of somebody who'd been through it a hundred times, though his shoulders were tense, his grip firm on his weapon. He'd turn check on her occasionally, his expression unreadable in the half-light. Reconciling this hardened fighter with the boy she'd once known was hard. The years had carved themselves into him, shaped him into someone she struggled to understand, but she still felt the old connection flickering beneath the surface—a bond time nor war had severed.

The silence stretched thick with anticipation until Jay, just behind Maia, muttered under his breath, his voice a strained whisper.

'Could these tunnels be any narrower? I feel like I'm in a damn coffin.'

'Keep it down,' Maia hissed without looking back. 'Sound travels.'

He shut up, but Ella sensed the nervous energy vibrating through him. His fingers fidgeted with a small device clipped to his belt, and she knew he was running through every scenario in his head. They'd all been briefed on the plan, but the reality of it was settling in, the enormity of what they were about to attempt hanging heavy over them.

As they continued, the air grew thicker, tinged with an acrid, metallic smell that made Ella's nose wrinkle. She kept her breathing shallow, the scent clawing at her lungs with every inhale. In the gloom, she noticed patches of strange, phosphorescent mould clinging to the walls, its faint greenish glow casting an eerie hue on their faces.

Billy turned, his face obscured, but she recognised the tightness in his expression, the way his eyes darted between her and the path ahead. 'You holding up?' he asked.

'I'm fine. Just... feels like we're walking into a trap.'

He glanced away, his gaze lingering on the shadowed corners of the passage. 'Maybe we are. But it's our only chance.'

She opened her mouth to reply, but a sudden noise froze her in place—a faint, distant hum that echoed through the tunnels, vibrating through the walls like a low, pulsing heartbeat. The group halted, everyone going still, their breaths suspended as they listened.

'What is that?' Erin whispered.

Aelix stepped forward, their expression inscrutable. 'Security drones. They monitor the outer perimeters of the fortress. We're close.'

Ella's stomach twisted, and she tightened her grip on her blaster, feeling its cold weight against her palm. The compound was just ahead, with it, the Key to Time. She could save her parents, her friends, everything she'd lost. But the thought was laced with fear; the Key's power was immense, and she knew it wasn't something to take lightly.

'Do they know we're here?' Jay asked.

Aelix shook their head, though the tension lines around their mouth suggested they weren't as confident as they wanted to appear. 'No. But we need to stay alert. Once we're inside, every step we make will be monitored. We won't have much time. One chance, that's all we'll get.'

Maia motioned for them to keep moving, and they continued forward, the drone's hum fading as they left the tunnel behind. The path sloped upwards, and Ella felt the air growing colder, sharper. Her thoughts raced as she followed the others, trying to focus, to drown out the doubts clawing at her mind. After several minutes, they reached an old, rusted gate blocking the end of the passageway. Maia inspected it, touching the corroded metal as she leaned in and examined the hinges.

'It hasn't been used in a long time,' she murmured, glancing at Aelix. 'Are you sure this is the right way?'

Aelix nodded. 'It leads to the lower levels of the fortress and the lift that will take us up. It was abandoned after they upgraded their entry points, but it still connects to the main corridors. We'll bypass most of their patrols this way.'

Maia focused on the team. 'Get ready. Once we're through, there's no going back.'

Jay stepped forward with a look of nervous excitement as he reached into his pack, producing a small handheld torch. 'Let me do the honours.' He grinned with a flash of bravado Ella assumed masked his fear.

Aelix moved closer to Ella. 'Are you sure you're prepared for this?'

She felt the enormity of what lay ahead. 'I don't think anyone can be prepared for something like this. But I have no choice.'

Aelix's eyes held a flicker of something—understanding, maybe, or respect. 'The Key... it's powerful. Dangerous. Once we're inside, you'll see things that might make you question why you're here. Remember your purpose, Ella. Hold on to it. The fortress tends to cloud the mind.'

She looked at them, her chest tightening. 'What does that mean?'

Aelix hesitated. 'The Key isn't just a machine. It's alive. It senses your thoughts and your intentions. It draws from them and feeds on them. It will try to twist you. Resist it.'

She grabbed Aelix's arm. 'You said your people found it floating in space hundreds of years ago.'

They nodded. 'Yes. That is what we are told. It took a long time for our scientists to understand what it is and master it, but they have total control of the Key now.'

'Do your people know what it is?'

Aelix shook their head. 'Not fully, no. It contains a previously unknown energy. But...'

'But what?'

'A few days ago, something changed in that energy. Before, it was like it lay sleeping. I think that's why the invaders could master its powers. Now, it's different. It seems it's waking up, and those near it are worried.'

'A few days ago,' she repeated. 'When I arrived here?'

'Yes,' they answered. 'You have a connection to it, Ella. What that is, I don't know.'

She gulped. 'Is that why you were waiting for Maia and me on the cliffs?'

'It was,' Aelix said, touching the symbol on his neck. 'I felt a change here. We all did. It led me to you.'

Ella gripped the weapon in her pocket. 'Do your people know about me?'

'The invaders understand that something has changed.'

She tried to control her breathing. 'So there could be other aliens searching for me?'

Aelix agreed. 'Yes.'

Before she could respond, Jay finished his work on the gate with a soft click, the rusted hinges creaking as it swung open, revealing a passage shrouded in darkness. The air that drifted out was cold, carrying a faint electrical hum that made Ella's skin itch.

Billy nodded. 'Let's move.'

They stepped through, entering the heart of enemy territory. It was narrow, claustrophobic, and her shoulders brushed against the walls as they pressed forward, her footsteps muffled against the ground. Her pulse increased, thundering, a wild rhythm that matched the steady thrum of machinery echoing from somewhere deeper within.

The tunnel opened into a cavernous chamber lined with alien symbols that glowed, casting an eerie light across the space. The glyphs pulsed, almost alive, shifting and swirling as if watching them. Ella shivered, drawn to the strange markings.

'What are those?' she whispered.

Aelix's eyes lingered on the symbols, their face shadowed. 'Guidance markers. They track movement and record memories. They're embedded in every part of the fortress. They'll know we're here now.'

A heavy silence followed those words, and Ella gripped her weapon, her palms damp with sweat.

Maia turned to the group, her voice low but steady. 'Stay close. No noise.' She faced Aelix. 'How do we get up?'

'Follow me,' they replied.

They moved through the chamber, the flickering light from the symbols casting distorted shadows that danced along the walls, making it hard to tell where the solid ground ended and the darkness began. Ella felt her mind pulling in strange directions, her thoughts slipping between fear and an eerie, inexplicable curiosity.

They reached the chamber's far end, where narrow stairs spiralled up. Maia hesitated, peering at Aelix. 'These steps are invisible outside?'

'Yes,' Aelix replied. 'My people never use this way. It's for the smaller machines to get in and out of the compound.'

'You mean there might be some of them in there with us?' Billy asked.

Aelix nodded. 'So be careful.'

As they stepped inside, the air grew colder, thicker, and the mechanical hum became a low, rhythmic beat that seemed to pulse in time with Ella's heartbeat. It surged through her bones.

At the top, they entered a long hallway with sleek metal panels covering the walls. The floor was smooth and reflective, and every step echoed down the length of the corridor, swallowed by the thick silence. Ella saw a massive set of doors at the far end, their surface etched with intricate alien designs that seemed to writhe in the dim light.

'That's it,' Aelix whispered. 'The entrance to the next levels.'

Ella's stomach twisted, a sick feeling settling deep within her. She knew this was it. This was the point of no return. Beyond those doors lay the Key, the heart of the alien fortress, and the power to change everything—or destroy it.

Chapter 14

The Fortress

Aelix signalled for them to stay low as they moved down a narrow corridor, the walls gleaming with an unnatural green glow. They hadn't yet entered the fortress's heart, but Ella sensed danger.

She gripped her weapon, senses on high alert, anticipating movement at any second. Behind her, she heard the soft shuffle of boots and steady breathing, though every sound felt too loud, too dangerous. Everywhere hummed with energy, as if the fortress was alive, watching them, waiting for them to make a mistake.

Aelix crouched low at the front. 'The first security checkpoint is up ahead. We'll need to bypass it without tripping the alarms.'

Jay followed beside Aelix. His fingers danced across the control panel embedded in the wall, assessing the system. He muttered something, and then his voice crackled through the comms. 'Looks like they've upgraded the locks. Give me a minute. Maybe two.'

Ella glanced at Billy, crouched beside her. She sensed the same nervous energy rolling off him that she was fighting to control. He gave her a reassuring nod, but his grip on his weapon was tight. His desperation to save his family had been simmering beneath the surface, and she understood its toll on him. She opened her mouth to say something—stay focused or we'll get through this—but the words felt empty in the face of the impending danger.

'Got it,' Jay hissed, as the control panel blinked green. The door slid open.

'Move,' Aelix ordered, and they filed through the doorway, their movements sharp and efficient, well-practised from countless skirmishes. But this was different. This wasn't just another hit-and-run mission against alien patrols. They were deep inside enemy territory now. One mistake, and they were all dead.

As they pressed deeper into the fortress, the corridors grew wider, the walls lined with strange glyphs that pulsed with energy. Ella felt the alien technology drumming beneath her, the building alive with power, with cold, mechanical intelligence.

You could cut the tension with a knife.

Zara spoke. 'We're sitting ducks here. I don't like it. This whole place feels wrong.'

'Keep it together,' Erin shot back. 'We knew what we were walking into.'

Zara didn't respond, but Ella recognised the doubt in her eyes. It wasn't just her, though. Everyone was on edge, nerves fraying as they ventured deeper into the fortress. Ella's breath came in short, shallow gasps as they moved from door to door, each a potential trap, her heart beating a frantic rhythm against her ribs.

Is this going to work?

The thought crept in despite her efforts to push it away. The mission had seemed straightforward—get in, retrieve the Key (or destroy it), get out—but now the alien monstrosity surrounded them, and doubt gnawed at her. What if Aelix was wrong? What if they couldn't reach the Key? What if the fortress were a death trap they'd never escape?

What if it was all a trap?

The Key – whatever it was – had been sleeping but awakened when she'd arrived from the past. Why? And were there other aliens tracking her right now?

She clenched her fists, trying to focus.

Stay sharp. Don't let fear control you.

Aelix stopped, raising a hand. The group froze. Up ahead, the corridor opened into a larger chamber, the air buzzing with the faint sound of machinery. Ella saw them then—patrolling machines, sleek and deadly, their metal limbs gleaming under the low lights. They moved with mechanical precision, scanning every corner of the room.

'Security drones,' Aelix whispered. 'We need a distraction.'

Jay nodded, pulling out a small device from his pack. 'I can overload their sensors and make it look like we're coming from the opposite direction. But we'll only have a few seconds to get through before they recalibrate.'

'Do it,' Maia ordered, focused on the machines.

Ella held her breath as he worked, the moments stretching out, every second feeling like an eternity. Jay flicked a switch and a shock of energy shot through the air. The drones paused, their sensors whirring as they shifted direction, drawn to an empty section.

'Now,' Aelix said.

They darted past the drones into the next hallway. Her heart was still going a mile a minute after they got through, nerves gripping her body with icy fingers. As they pushed forward, the atmosphere grew heavier. The fortress was a maze of endless corridors, each more foreboding than the last. Ella felt the dread settling in, creeping up like a shadow she couldn't shake. The walls seemed to shrink around them, the oppressive silence broken only by the faint hum of alien technology.

'How much further?' Billy asked, his frustration bubbling to the surface.

Aelix glanced back. 'Not far. We're approaching the central hub. Once we get past it, we'll be closer to the Key.'

Billy muttered something, but Ella didn't have time to respond. Up ahead, the corridor widened into a massive chamber, larger than the ones they'd passed before. And it was filled with alien soldiers.

Aelix cursed, signalling for them to halt. The invaders were armoured, their bodies encased in sleek, silver exoskeletons, weapons slung across their backs. They moved with an unnatural precision, their eyes glowing under their helmets as they patrolled the chamber.

'We can't fight all of them,' Erin whispered. 'There's too many.'

Aelix nodded. 'We'll have to go around. There should be another route through the maintenance tunnels.'

But before they could move, there was a sudden clang, metal against metal. Ella's heart dropped as she saw Zara stumble, her boot catching on a loose panel. The noise echoed through the chamber, and the aliens turned, guns locking onto the group.

'Run!' Aelix shouted.

The next moments were a blur. Ella sprinted down the corridor as gunfire erupted behind them. She heard Erin barking orders, the crackle of energy weapons as they fired at the soldiers. She refused to look back, focusing on the path ahead and staying alive. Someone screamed behind her. She wasn't sure who it was, but it didn't matter. Somebody had fallen. And there was no time to stop, no time to mourn.

They burst through a door, slamming it shut behind them, the sounds of battle muffled by the thick metal. Ella leaned against the wall, struggling to breathe. Her chest burned, and her legs trembled. She glanced around. Most of the group had made it - but not all.

Zara was missing. So was Erin.

Billy stood a few feet away, his face pale. 'We lost them. They're gone.'

Ella swallowed the lump in her throat, trying to push back the guilt, the grief. They couldn't afford to fall apart. Not when they were so close.

'We keep moving,' Aelix said, his voice cold and emotionless. 'There's no time to grieve. We finish the mission. We won't get another chance after this.'

Tensions rippled through the group. Zara had been one of their best fighters, and Erin had been their strategist. Without them, the path ahead felt even more dangerous. Suspicion swirled in the air, unspoken but heavy.

'What if we can't do this?' Billy's voice was low, but its tremor was impossible to miss. 'We've lost too many. Maybe this mission was doomed from the start.'

Ella's heart clenched. She'd been thinking the same, doubts gnawing at her since they entered the fortress. She saw it in the faces of the others—the uncertainty, the fear. They'd worked so hard, but now that they were inside, it felt impenetrable, invincible.

'Billy, don't—' she started, but he cut her off.

'No, Ella. I'm serious. We keep pushing forward, and

more of us are going to die. For what? The Key? Do we even know if we can get to it? What if it's all in vain?'

His voice was rising, the anger and desperation in it palpable. Ella was at a loss for words. She felt it too—the creeping doubt, the fear that maybe they'd journeyed so far for nothing.

'And your family?' she said.

Anguish gripped his face. 'I'll talk to the aliens, bargain with them.' His lips trembled as he glanced around them. 'I was wrong to come. If they discover me here, they'll kill Jessica and the girls.'

'The fortress is planting doubt in your mind,' Aelix said. 'You must fight it.'

Ella dug her nails into her palms. 'What?'

Aelix looked at her. 'This is a living structure. Now you are inside it, it is reaching into your minds, trying to manipulate you.'

Before she could reply, the floor shook, a deafening boom echoing through the chamber. Ella's heart seized as the force of the explosion threw her off her feet. She hit the ground hard; the wind knocked out of her as debris rained down around them.

'Billy!' she screamed, scrambling up, but thick smoke obscured everything, the stink of burning metal filling her lungs. She couldn't see him—couldn't see anything through the haze.

Ella's panic surged as she stumbled forward, her hands clawing at the billowing cloud, searching for him.

But Billy was gone.

Chapter 15

The Fight

Smoke choked the air, thick and bitter as it billowed through the hallway, clawing at Ella's throat. She pressed her sleeve against her mouth, trying to steady her breathing, but her lungs burned, and her heart was ready to explode. Every instinct screamed for her to run, to push on, but the fortress was a labyrinth of gleaming metal walls, each corridor indistinguishable from the last.

And it was alive.

She stumbled forward, eyes stinging, her gaze darting through the haze for any sign of Billy. They'd been scattered in the blast—his name had barely left her lips before the smoke consumed him, leaving her stranded in the chaos.

'Billy!' she called, her voice absorbed by the heavy silence that had replaced the loud noise of the explosion. The fortress groaned around Ella, sealing her off and removing any sense of direction. She couldn't tell where she was or even if she was moving closer to—or further from—her team.

The lights lining the corridor flickered, casting twisted shadows that seemed to move with her, slithering over the sleek, metallic surface of the walls. The alien symbols pulsed, their glow a sickening green, bathing everything in an eerie, unnatural light. She forced herself to keep her eyes sharp, even as her mind screamed to stop, to hide, to—

Her foot caught on something, and she went sprawling, hitting the wall. Pain shot through her shoulder; she looked down, and bile rose in her throat.

A helmet. Human-made, cracked and blood-streaked, lying abandoned on the floor. She recognised it as Erin's. The fortress had swallowed her, just as it seemed it was doing to her.

Focus, she told herself, swallowing her fear. She forced herself forward, feeling her pulse throbbing in her ears, her fingers cold and tight around her blaster. The corridor twisted and turned in impossible angles, an omniscient presence watching her every move.

A soft humming reached her ears, a rhythmic, pulsing sound that vibrated through the building, filling her bones with an unsettling, uncomfortable energy. She rounded a corner, stopping short, when she saw a dimly lit room ahead, the walls lined with transparent glass stretched from floor to ceiling. Behind the glass, human figures lay suspended, held upright by metal restraints, their faces hidden by thick tubes vibrating with a faint, sickly green fluid, bodies thin and pale, covered in strange marks that shimmered under the glass's dim light.

She pressed a trembling hand to the surface, peering closer, her skin crawling as she realised that the people were still, yet somehow alive—barely, but alive. She saw their chests moving, shallow breaths that rose and fell in an unnatural, mechanical rhythm as if the fortress were breathing for them.

'What...?' Her voice cracked, the horror settling in her chest like ice.

As if in answer, a door on the far side of the room slid open, and an alien stepped inside. Its skin glowed, a sickly yellow hue that caught the light and seemed to ripple as if it wasn't flesh at all but some translucent, organic armour. Ella froze, watching as it approached one of the humans behind the glass, pressing a hand to a panel beside the tube.

The fluid in the tube surged, turning a deeper, darker green, and the body convulsed, limbs twitching as if electrified. A strangled sound escaped Ella's throat, and she covered her mouth, desperate to keep quiet, to remain hidden. The alien's head tilted, observing the body with a clinical detachment that disgusted her. She sensed its disregard, its utter indifference to the life before it.

She backed away, inching towards the door, the desire to flee warring with the instinct to stay silent, invisible. But she wasn't paying attention, bumping into a table and sending equipment crashing onto the floor.

The alien's head jerked at Ella, eyes narrowing as it fixed on her, cold and unfeeling. Its mouth opened, and a faint clicking sound filled the air, a noise that made her skin crawl, like nails scraping against metal.

She turned, bolting down the corridor. The rhythmic hum increased, an insistent beat that matched her frantic pulse as she ran, twisting and turning through the fortress's maze-like halls. The lights flickered faster, casting disorienting shadows, making it harder to tell where she was going. She heard something behind her—a faint mechanical whirring that grew louder with each step. She kept moving, her lungs burning, her vision blurring as she stumbled through the corridors, desperate for any sign of an exit.

'Ella, you can't just keep running!' The voice echoed in

her mind, an old memory, but she shoved it aside, focusing on the present, on the metallic walls that seemed to close in on her, tighter and tighter with each step.

Up ahead, she spotted another door, different from the others—a thick, reinforced slab of metal with alien symbols carved into its surface. She pressed her hand to the panel beside it, praying it would open, but it flashed red, denying her access. The whirring sound grew closer, the echo of mechanical footsteps reverberating down the corridor, slow and deliberate, as if the creature knew she had nowhere to go.

She backed away from the door, her breathing ragged, her mind racing as she searched for any way out. She sensed the presence behind her, its stony gaze fixed on her, and her fear sharpened, her body tensing as she prepared to fight, to do whatever it took to—

A hand clamped down on her shoulder, and she twisted around to see not an alien but a human—Jay, his face drawn and pale, his eyes wide with terror.

'Quiet!' he hissed, pulling her into a small alcove, out of sight of the corridor. He touched his lips, and she held back her questions to keep her breathing low.

The footsteps passed, the creature's shadow stretching over the walls, long and distorted, before it moved on, vanishing down another passageway.

'What happened to the others?' she asked him.

Jay shrugged. 'I don't know. It all went to shit, and I couldn't see anything in the smoke.'

She nodded, swallowing hard, her heart still pounding. 'We have to find them.'

He peered over her shoulder. 'What are they doing here? The people behind the glass?'

Ella shook her head, her expression haunted. 'Experiments. They take humans, test them and drain them. The aliens are studying us, using us for fuel, I think.'

Jay grimaced. 'Fuel? They're using people as fuel?'

'Yes,' she said, her guts burning.

Before he could respond, a loud, blaring siren filled the corridor, its piercing tone reverberating through the walls.

'They know we're here,' Jay muttered. 'We have to move.'

He grabbed her arm, pulling her through the maze of corridors, their footsteps swallowed by the screaming alarm. They moved quickly, Ella's senses heightened, her pulse a relentless beat as they weaved through the fortress, dodging patrols and slipping through narrow passageways that seemed to stretch forever.

But it wasn't enough.

A shadowy shape loomed at the end of the corridor, blocking their path. The alien soldier was taller than the others, its skin a dark, glistening yellow, with strange, metallic bands encircling its limbs. Its eyes glowed with an unnatural light as it lifted a long, serrated weapon, pointing it at them.

Jay raised his gun, but he was too slow. The alien struck first, moving with a blurred speed, its weapon slicing through the air with a sickening hiss. Jay cried out, his body jerking as the blade cut deep, collapsing in a heap beside her.

Ella staggered back, her mind blank with terror, her hands slick with sweat as she brought her blaster up, firing at the alien. The shots hit the creature's armour, sparking off the metal surface, but it didn't flinch; its gaze locked on her, cold and calculating.

She turned to run, but the creature moved too fast, blocking her path, its weapon ready. She stumbled, falling against the wall, her blaster slipping from her. A cold, metallic hand closed around her arm, the grip like a vice, holding her in place. She struggled, kicking and thrashing, but the alien's hold tightened, its gaze unyielding. It leaned closer, its breath hot and foul, smelling of something sharp and acidic. Its eyes narrowed, its voice a low, guttural growl.

'Human,' it hissed, the word a mockery in its mouth. 'You are nothing.'

Ella's vision blurred, her body going limp as the creature's grip pressed into her flesh, her thoughts slipping away, consumed by the darkness gathering at the edges of her mind. The last thing she saw was its cold, alien gaze, watching her with the detached curiosity of a predator before the world faded into blackness.

Chapter 16

The General

Ella jerked awake, her hands restrained as something dragged her along a corridor. The eerie glow of the green, pulsating lights lining the walls bathed everything in an unsettling, nauseating hue. Her boots scraped against the smooth, polished floor each time she moved, echoing through the cavernous hallways as two alien guards flanked her, their mechanical armour whirring with every move.

Others were ahead of her, more prisoners, though she couldn't determine who they were. Her skull throbbed, her pulse quickening with each passing moment, dragged deeper into the heart of enemy territory. She glanced sideways, trying to see if Billy, Aelix, or the rest were there. Her heart sank as she saw them, heads lowered, arms bound in front of them, walking silently. Billy's expression was stern, his jaw clenched.

The corridor opened into a vast, high-ceilinged chamber that stretched forever, the walls lined with sleek, dark panels glistening with strange technology. More guards were stationed at every corner, their luminous eyes watching the prisoners as they passed. Ella's skin prickled under their gaze, but her attention was drawn to something far worse than what was happening to her. To her left were people in a row of transparent, vertical chambers. Their bodies hung limp inside the glass-like structures, suspended in glowing fluid. Wires and tubes were connected to their limbs, heads, and chests. They were barely recognisable as humans anymore. Their faces were slack, eyes closed, mouths open as if in a deep, unnatural sleep. But the machinery surrounding them, the grotesque fusion of flesh and metal, sent a shiver of horror down Ella's spine.

She stared in disbelief, her mouth dry, as they passed more of the chambers, each filled with humans. Some of them twitched, their muscles thrashing in response to whatever horrific experiments they endured. The cold, sterile smell of the room and the machinery's faint hum made her stomach turn.

'These are people,' she whispered, her voice shaking with disbelief and anger.

Aelix, walking just ahead of her, glanced back, his expression grim. 'This is how they study humans, how they learn. The Key to Time allows them to manipulate history, but they need subjects. Test cases.'

Billy's face was a mask of horror as he muttered, 'We're nothing but lab rats to them.'

The guards gave no sign they'd heard anything. They continued forward, unbothered by the human suffering. Ella swallowed the bile rising in her throat. She was helpless, bound and trapped within a fortress of nightmares. As they walked, she felt the weight of every step, the walls pressing in, suffocating her. The air was heavy and thick with the oppressive presence of alien control. The building was a marvel of design—cold, sleek, efficient—but no humanity existed. No soul.

Ahead, the corridor opened into a massive hall, the ceiling disappearing into the shadows above. A towering figure flanked by several invaders stood at the far end. Ella shivered as she stared at him.

He grinned at her. 'My name is General Valtor.'

His presence was commanding, tall and imposing. His armour was sleek and alien in design, but unlike the other soldiers, his face was visible—human-like, with sharp features. His skin was a pale yellow, almost translucent, his eyes glowing with a piercing blue light that cut through the gloom. His countenance was cold and calculating as he watched them approach, his hands clasped behind his back.

Guards dragged the prisoners to him and shoved them to their knees. Ella's body ached, but she forced herself to stay still, to keep her expression neutral despite the tension coursing through her veins. She sensed Billy tense beside her, his muscles coiled, ready to fight if given the chance, but there was no point. Not now.

Valtor studied them, his lips curling into a faint, predatory smile. 'So,' he said, his voice deep, smooth, and laced with a sinister edge, 'these are the so-called rebels who have caused so much trouble.'

His eyes lingered on Ella for a long moment.

'You're welcome,' she said.

He ignored her, turning to Aelix. 'We must make an example of the traitor.'

'I'm loyal to life,' Aelix replied.

'It's fair to say,' Valtor continued, stepping closer, 'you've proven to be quite the thorn in our side. But I can't say I'm surprised.'

Ella glared at him, her jaw clenched. 'You should let us go.'

Valtor tilted his head, studying her. 'You're the one who fell through time, aren't you?' His voice was almost mocking. 'I've been waiting for this moment.'

Ella's heart skipped a beat. How did he know? How could he know?

'I see the confusion in your eyes,' Valtor continued. 'You've been wondering why you were transported through the ages, haven't you? Why it was you and not someone else? What connection do you have to the Key to Time?' He stepped closer, casting a shadow over her. 'We shall find out.'

Ella's pulse quickened. She gritted her teeth. 'You might not like what you discover.'

Valtor crouched before her, his glowing eyes locking onto hers. 'The Key to Time isn't only a tool for manipulating the past. It is the heart of our control. With it, we bend history to our will. We master the flow of events, ensuring our empire reigns supreme.' He reached out, almost touching her, but stopped just short. 'But there's a unique quality about you, child. The Key heard you when you arrived.' He touched the symbol on his neck. 'And it cried out to us all – it spoke to us all.'

Ella swallowed hard, her throat tight. She wanted to recoil, to back away from him, but she couldn't move. His words stung like a hook, pulling her deeper into a dark realisation.

'Saying what?' she asked.

Valtor caressed her cheek, and she shivered. 'Patience, child.'

'Get on with it,' she said.

He grinned. 'You were pulled through time because of

your connection to the Key. It responds to those who have the power to influence it. You, young one, are one of those people. Now we have to find out why.'

Her mind spun, trying to process everything. The idea she was tied to this alien weapon, this instrument of destruction and control, made little sense. But deep down, something about his words rang true, which terrified her.

'My name is Ella,' she spat.

Valtor stood again, towering over her. 'You see, the Key isn't just a tool for domination. It can also be a mechanism for salvation for you, Ella. Imagine what you could do with the power to control time. Imagine the people you could save. The lives you could change.'

She gasped. He offered her everything she wanted—the chance to rewrite the past and rescue her family, friends, and the world. But at what cost?

Billy growled under his breath, his fists clenched. 'Don't listen to him, Ella. He's lying.'

Valtor's gaze flickered to Billy, and a cruel smile tugged at the corner of his lips. 'Ah, the man who lost everything. You imagine you know pain, don't you? You think you understand loss.' He leaned down, his voice a low whisper. 'But you haven't seen true suffering yet. Do you want to know what happened to your wife and children?'

'Where are they?' Billy screamed.

Ella's chest tightened as she glanced at Billy. His face was pale, his eyes burning with anger and desperation. She realised the toll this was taking on him, the weight of his pain threatening to crush him.

'Why, they're with all the other batteries,' Valtor said.

Tears streamed down Billy's face. 'Batteries?'

'Yes, the Key needs constant energy. Our people

sufficed for a while, but you humans contain more electricity in your brains than other animals.'

Billy collapsed, pushing his head into the floor, sobbing.

Ella's heart broke for him. She bit into her top lip and glared at Valtor. 'You're the animal.'

He straightened, his attention returning to her. 'You're different from the other humans, child. You've travelled through time. Even with the Key, we can't do that. How did you?'

Ella tasted her blood. 'I'll never tell you.'

Valtor moved forward, stamping on Billy's back, forcing him into the floor. 'I could torture your friends. Would that loosen your tongue?'

'Don't do it, Ella,' Billy gasped.

The general removed his foot, focusing on Ella. 'No, I'm sure you wouldn't weaken for that. My scientists want to cut you up, child, to slice apart your brain while you're awake.' He shook his head. 'They are fools. We have to take a gentler road with you. I can give you what you want. A home in this new world. A place of power. All you have to do is join us.' He glanced at Aelix. 'I'll even let you keep your pet.'

The room closed around her, the air thick with tension. Her mind raced, torn between the temptation of his offer and the horrifying reality of what it would mean. The thought of aligning herself with monsters and using their power for gain was sickening. But the idea of turning down the chance to change everything, to save the people she loved...

'Ella,' Billy's voice broke through her thoughts. 'Don't.'

She looked at him, his eyes pleading. She saw the fear in them—the fear of losing her and what she might become if she took Valtor's offer.

Ella paused to catch her breath. She'd been through too much to let some alien tyrant mess with her. She was hurting, but she knew she had to find a better way to deal with it.

She met Valtor's gaze. 'I'm not like you. I won't be a pawn in your game.'

For a moment, there was silence. His smile faded, replaced by a cold, calculating expression. He regarded her for a long time, his eyes narrowing.

'Very well,' he said, his voice laced with menace. 'You've made a grave mistake.'

Ella held his gaze, refusing to show any fear. 'We'll see.'

Valtor straightened, his expression unreadable. 'Take them away.'

The guards moved, gripping Ella and the others, pulling them to their feet. Ella's heart sank as they dragged her from the room, but she didn't look back. She wouldn't give Valtor the satisfaction.

Ella's mind ached as they were led away, deeper into the fortress. She'd defied him.

But at what cost?

Chapter 17

The Prison

The prison cell was small, a pale green glow of an energy barrier shimmering in the doorway. Ella sat against the cold metal wall, her knees pulled to her chest, arms resting on them. The room was silent except for the faint hum of alien machinery in the distance. She heard others shifting in their cells nearby, their soft murmurs just audible over the constant vibe of the fortress.

Opposite her, Billy paced the length of his cell, fists clenched in frustration. 'We have to get out of here. We can't sit around and wait for whatever they have planned.'

Ella didn't respond, her head reeling from her encounter with Valtor. The offer he'd made her echoed in her mind. She could still see his cold, calculating eyes, the cruel smile that had played across his lips when she'd refused him.

'You're the key to something bigger,' Valtor had said, his voice smooth and venomous. 'And we will find out what it is, one way or another.'

She shivered. She'd been pulled through time and space, ripped from her world, and now these aliens—these invaders—believed she held some secret tied to the Key. But she didn't know what it was. She didn't understand why she'd been displaced, why time had chosen her.

Was it connected to the Light inside her?

But that was all gone.

Wasn't it?

Ella closed her eyes, searching deep inside her for the energy she'd used before – looking for the Light she'd stolen from Pandora.

It wasn't there.

She opened her eyes and peered at Billy. 'He might have been lying about your family, Billy. That general – Valtor – was messing with us. You can't trust what he said.'

Billy glanced at Aelix in the cell near Ella. 'It doesn't matter now. We've lost half the team and didn't get close to the Key.' He punched the wall, and she saw his blood stain the surface. 'We were screwed before we even began.'

Ella turned to Aelix. 'What do you know about Valtor?'

Aelix looked at her; their face shadowed with an unfamiliar expression—something close to dread. They sat cross-legged on the floor of their cell, the green glow from the energy barrier casting eerie shadows on their pale, angular features.

'Valtor is more dangerous than you can imagine. He's not just a general; he's one of the most feared leaders of my kind. He controls the army, the experiments, the Key... and the sacrifices.' They hesitated, their gaze dropping to the floor as if the words were too heavy to say.

Ella's stomach twisted. 'Sacrifices? What do you mean?'

Aelix's face remained unreadable, but there was a flash of something in their eyes—regret, perhaps, or a haunted resignation. 'The Key to Time is not a machine in the sense you might think. It's a living construct bound to our people by a contract of energy. It must be fed organic life to keep it functioning, to give it the ability to manipulate time.'

Billy had stopped pacing, his fists dropping as he absorbed the weight of Aelix's words. 'So the rumours... about using humans as fuel... they're true?'

Ella didn't mention what she'd seen when they were separated, though the images were seared into her brain.

'Yes,' Aelix said, avoiding his gaze. 'That's why your people are captured and sent to the compounds. Valtor oversees it all, ensuring there's a constant supply.' Their words were strained, as if each one took something from them to say aloud.

Ella's head reeled, her throat tight. The horror of it all settled over her like a suffocating blanket. The fortress was nothing more than a processing machine for human lives—a place where people like her, people like Billy's family, were drained of everything to fuel a monstrous device. She felt a fresh surge of anger, her fingers curling into fists as she looked toward Aelix.

'And you let this happen?' she demanded, her voice sharp, laced with a bitterness she didn't hide. 'All this time... you knew.'

Aelix's head dropped lower. 'I was once part of it, yes. I won't deny that. But things change, Ella. You learn what it costs and what it means. I left, and it's cost me everything.' Their gaze met hers, a haunted look in their eyes. 'You think I don't regret every moment?'

Billy pressed his palms against the wall of his cell. 'Regret doesn't bring people back. It doesn't save my family.'

Ella's heart ached for Billy and his family, trapped in this nightmare, reduced to nothing more than fuel for a machine. The thought made her sick, her skin prickling with a rage she could barely contain.

'I won't let it end like this,' she said, her voice shaking with anger and resolve. 'I don't care what Valtor wants or what he thinks he knows about me. We're getting out of here. And we're going to destroy that Key.'

She couldn't use it to return home when she knew the cost.

Footsteps echoed down the corridor, growing louder with each passing moment. Ella tensed, her eyes flicking toward the doorway, where the shimmering energy barrier kept them trapped. The others went silent, listening as the steps stopped outside.

The barrier flickered, then disappeared. The door slid open, revealing Valtor, standing tall and imposing, flanked by two guards. His expression was calm, but a coldness in his eyes bothered her.

'So,' he said, his voice as smooth as oil, dripping with a cruel amusement, 'you've had time to consider my offer.'

Ella glared at him. 'What do you want with us?'

Valtor's smile widened, and he took a slow, deliberate step forward, his gaze pressing down on her like claws around her throat. 'Want? My dear girl, I want nothing from you. I already have you.' His focus shifted to Aelix, a glimmer of satisfaction in his eyes. 'And you, my brave collaborator. You've been quite the nuisance, haven't you? All those years, working hard to undermine us from the inside.'

Aelix clenched their fists, blazing with defiance. 'I've only just begun.'

Valtor gave a low chuckle, the sound cold and devoid of genuine humour. 'I admire your spirit; it's entertaining.' He shifted his attention back to Ella, his eyes narrowing as he studied her, as though she were a puzzle he intended to solve piece by piece.

'I've heard interesting things about you, Ella,' he continued, his tone soft, almost reverent. 'You see, we've collected humans from many worlds several times. But none quite like you. You don't belong here, do you?'

She glared at him, refusing to let him get under her skin. 'No,' she said. 'But that doesn't mean I'll help you.'

Valtor's smile didn't waver. 'Oh, I don't need you to *do* anything. I only require you to exist. You see, you're an extraordinary anomaly. And special anomalies attract attention.' He gestured to the dark, humming walls around them. 'This fortress, the Key, all of it—it senses you, Ella. It knows you're here, and it's curious.'

A chill ran through her, but she kept her face neutral. 'I don't know what you're talking about.'

'Oh, but you will.' His gaze sharpened, a gleam of triumph flashing in his eyes. 'You see, the Key has been waiting for something... someone, to unlock its full potential. I believe you may be that person. All you need is a little persuasion.'

'Fuck you!' Billy said.

Valtor ignored him, stepping closer to the barrier of Ella's cell, the faint glow casting his features in an even more sinister light. 'Imagine, Ella. Time itself at your command. The power to change fate, to erase entire lifetimes with a mere thought. Doesn't that tempt you?'

She forced herself to hold his gaze as her heart hammered in her chest. 'And what would you do with that kind of power? Rewrite the world to suit your whims. Play god?'

He laughed, a dangerous glint in his expression. 'Isn't that what every being desires at their core? Power is the only truth, the only constant. Your species' weakness is in your refusal to see it.'

Aelix shifted, their expression unreadable as they met Ella's gaze. There was something in their expression—a silent warning, perhaps, or an apology. She couldn't be sure, but it grounded her and gave her the strength to hold firm.

Ella glared at Valtor, her voice steady, defiant. 'Whatever you think I am, whatever you want from me, you won't get it.'

He tilted his head, a faint smirk tugging at his lips. 'We'll see. Everyone has a breaking point. Even those with a spark of Light buried inside them.'

Her eyes widened, but she masked her reaction. 'What?'

Valtor's smile widened, his gaze gleaming with something dark and triumphant. 'Oh, Ella... I know far more than you realise. Your past, your potential. You and I are connected in ways you cannot yet comprehend. But you will.'

He stepped back, his eyes flicking over each of them with a cold satisfaction. 'Enjoy your time here. You'll soon discover what happens to those who resist.' He glanced at Billy, a mockery of sympathy in his expression. 'And don't worry, brave human. You might even get to see your family again.'

Billy's fists clenched, his jaw tight with barely contained fury. 'I swear if you've hurt them—'

Valtor raised a hand, silencing him with a mocking smile. 'Hurt them? Oh no. They're quite alive, for now. But life is fragile, especially here. I'd tread carefully if I were you.'

'Leave him alone!' Ella shouted.

Valtor grinned. 'And if I don't?'

Ella's jaw clenched, but she didn't back down. 'I have

no idea how I ended up here. I know nothing about time travel.'

Valtor's smile faded, replaced by a look of cold calculation. 'Then you give me no alternative.'

He turned away, motioning to the guards. 'Prepare her for transport to the lab. We'll begin the experiments immediately.'

'No!' Billy shouted, stepping forward. 'You can't do this!'

Valtor glanced over his shoulder, his expression indifferent. 'I can do whatever I want. This is my world now.'

Then the aliens came for her.

Chapter 18

Echoes of Time

The guards hauled Ella down a twisting hallway, their hands like nails in her arms, dragging her deeper into the fortress. The passage was dark and metallic, and she felt she would disappear. Her heart was racing, but she kept quiet. She had to keep it together, even though she was freaking out inside.

They turned a corner, then another, until they reached a heavy door marked with alien symbols shimmering a sickly green that twisted her stomach. One of the guards placed a hand on a panel beside it, and the entrance slid open, revealing a cavernous room bathed in an eerie, shifting light. Ella trudged along, her feet dragging, stopping as she lifted her gaze.

She gasped.

In the centre was a floating stone—small, no larger than her fist, rough and unassuming, yet it pulsed with a faint, ethereal glow that rippled outward in glistening waves. Hovering around it were several people, suspended in mid-air, connected by thin beams of light that flowed from their skulls to the stone's surface. The lights flickered in shades of pale blue and violet, each beam like a tendril holding them in place, binding them in a web of energy. Their bodies were limp, heads tilted back, eyes closed, expressions frozen in a twisted mixture of peace and agony.

Ella's stomach churned, a cold horror washing over her as she watched the slow rise and fall of their ribs, the way their limbs hung lifelessly, the faint tremors that rippled through them with every pulse of the stone.

'Beautiful, isn't it?'

Valtor's smooth and oily voice slid into the silence, making her skin crawl. He stood near her, fixated on the scene before them, a twisted satisfaction in his eyes.

Ella forced herself to turn from the floating figures and look at him, her jaw clenched. 'Beautiful? This is monstrous.'

Valtor's lips curved into a faint smile. 'Is it? Or is it simply... inevitable? My people discovered this centuries ago, drifting alone in the vastness of space, like a seed waiting to be planted. We recognised its power immediately, though it took us years to unlock its secrets.' He gestured to the stone. 'The Key to Time. As far as we know, it is the only one of its kind. A device that can reach into every future, each potential reality, all for the price of organic matter.'

The bile rose in her throat. 'You're using their brains to power it? To see the future?'

He inclined his head as if discussing something as mundane as a change in the weather. 'Precisely. The human brain is remarkably adaptive, more so than any other species we've encountered. Once we established the connection, it became clear that human neurons, when properly harnessed, could serve as conduits for the Key's visions. The more minds connected, the clearer the future becomes.'

Ella's eyes drifted back to the floating people, seeing a young girl, maybe sixteen, her long hair spilling around her, her features drawn and pale. The girl's fingers twitched, a faint tremor that made Ella shiver. She was alive, trapped in a nightmare she couldn't escape.

Valtor continued, oblivious to the horror on Ella's face. 'The Key lets us see all possible futures and predict every decision and action. It's how we remain one step ahead of your people and anticipate and counter every pathetic attempt to resist.' He grinned at her. 'It's how we knew you were coming here.'

Ella's fists clenched, her voice a low tremor. 'You're killing them.'

'Not quite.' His tone was almost amused, as if her revulsion was a minor inconvenience. 'They live as long as the Key requires them to. Their consciousness fades, replaced by a state of perpetual dreaming - a painless existence.'

She felt the bile rise again. 'Is that supposed to make this better? You're using people as fuel, tearing apart their minds to keep your precious Key running.'

Valtor shrugged, his focus shifting to the stone. 'It's not personal, Ella. It's survival. Progress. Would you prefer the chaos that would ensue if we allowed your people free will? You were already destroying this planet before we arrived.'

She took a step back, her fists shaking at her sides. 'Free will? You've stolen their lives, stripped away any choice they had. You're a parasite.'

Valtor's smile faded. 'Careful, Ella. You may not appreciate our methods, but you should respect the power of the Key. It has brought order and stability. Our society has flourished under its guidance. Without it, we would be as weak and scattered as your people.'

She looked at the stone, a dark hatred building within her. 'All you've done is destroy.'

He watched her, his eyes narrowing. 'I'd expect such a limited perspective from a human. But you... you are different, Ella. Special.' His tone softened, a glint of curiosity in his gaze. 'There's something in you that calls to the Key that even my people haven't been able to replicate. That's why I brought you here.'

She stiffened, every muscle in her body tensing. 'I have nothing to give you.'

'Oh, but you do.' He stepped closer, his eyes gleaming with a dangerous intent. 'You see, the Key is not just a tool for looking forward. It can also reach backwards into the past. Imagine rewriting history, changing the fabric of reality. Isn't there something you'd like to undo? Some tragic mistake you'd prefer to erase?'

The words cut into her, sharp and insidious. Images flashed through her mind—her family, her friends, the life she'd lost. The possibility tugged at her like a dark temptation, whispering of all the things she could bring back, all the people she could save.

Wasn't that why she was there – to change this *future* and return home?

But beneath that pull, she felt a chill, a cold warning that froze her bones.

'I don't trust you. I don't trust this... thing.' She gestured to the Key, the disgust clear in her voice. 'All you want is power. Control. And you'll say anything to get it.'

His expression remained impassive, but his eyes gleamed with a faint, chilling amusement. 'You're right, Ella. I want power. But I don't need to lie to you to get it.'

He motioned to the floating bodies, his gaze sweeping over them with a detached indifference. 'This is the price of progress, the foundation of everything we have built. And with your help, the Key's power could be limitless.'

'How many times do I have to say I won't help you?'

He laughed. 'My mistake. I must have given you the impression that your help would be voluntary.' He nodded to the guards, who pushed her towards the Key. 'Once it connects to your brain, imagine all the possibilities it will open to us.'

She tried to struggle, kicking out, but it was useless. As they inched her closer to the glowing artefact, she saw more faces of the enslaved humans, gasping at recognition: Commander Chen, Jax and Amari floated next to each other. Then she saw Billy's family, his wife and two daughters.

Ella finally gave up in those alien arms, her body relaxing even though her mind screamed. The Key to Time cast an ethereal glow that danced across the walls. She peered at the artefact, her breath shallow. The Key pulsed with an internal rhythm, a mesmerising dance of light and shadow that seemed alive. Each pulse of its illumination felt like a heartbeat reverberating through the chamber and into her core.

Then something shot out of it and into her head. A jolt of energy surged through her, making her stagger as the guards released her. The walls around her blurred into a vortex of shifting colours, pulling her into a chaotic sea of possibilities. Her heart raced from the disorienting sensation and the overwhelming realisation of what was about to unfold.

The chamber dissolved into a frantic swirl, and she was no longer in the fortress but suspended in a boundless expanse. The sky was a tumultuous canvas of purples, oranges, and blues, twisting and merging into an ever-changing panorama. The ground was translucent, rippling like disturbed water, reflecting the swirling sky.

Ella looked around, her senses overwhelmed by the vastness and surreal quality. She was no longer bound by time and space, drifting through the fabric of countless potential futures. Her mind, usually so focused and determined, was now a vessel for the potential the Key to Time had unlocked.

'Are you ready to see the possibilities?' someone whispered in her ear.

Before she could reply, radiant hope was the first vision unfurled before her. The world she saw was a testament to the resistance's success. Cities that had been battlegrounds were now bustling with activity. Skyscrapers, though scarred, stood tall and proud. Green spaces that had once been barren now teemed with life, children playing and laughing under the watchful eyes of their parents.

Ella saw herself amidst this thriving world, standing with Billy, Aelix, and the rest of the team. They were smiling, their faces lit with a profound sense of relief and joy. An aura of accomplishment and renewal filled the air. The vision was a utopian dream, a snapshot of what could be achieved if they succeeded in their mission. Billy's family were there, along with thousands of others, living perfect lives.

As Ella moved through this possibility, seeing people working together, their efforts focused on rebuilding and healing. The sense of unity was palpable, a collective determination to create something better from the ashes of their previous world. Ella's heart swelled with the beauty of this future, contrasting the grim reality she'd known.

Yet even in this hopeful vision, shadows lingered. Alien technology lay dormant, hidden within the infrastructure. The threat was not gone; it had retreated, waiting for another opportunity. Ella felt a pang of unease. The future was brighter, but the seeds of potential conflict remained, a reminder that their fight wasn't over. She reached out to touch it, to grasp Billy's hand, but he shimmered, and everything vanished into a swirling, cold mist.

The following vision was a chilling contrast. The world she beheld was a wasteland ravaged by the aftermath of the alien invasion. Dark clouds choked the sky; the ground was a desolate expanse of scorched earth and rubble. The remnants of once-grand cities lay in ruins, their buildings broken and overrun by twisted metal and shattered glass.

Ella saw herself wandering through this devastated landscape, her face lined with exhaustion and despair. The grief was overwhelming. The resistance had failed, the Key was lost, and the aliens had tightened their grip on Earth. The world was a ghost of its former self, haunted by the echoes of what could have been.

The vision revealed the suffering of humanity, their faces gaunt and hollow, their hope extinguished. She saw her allies—Billy, Aelix, Maia—each marked by the toll of their failure: broken spirits, their resolve shattered. The scene was a haunting reminder of the stakes of their mission and the dire consequences of an inevitable defeat.

Then, another future emerged, brimming with treachery and deceit. Ella saw a grand command centre, its sleek, high-tech surfaces cold and impersonal. Valtor was there with his commanders, studying scenes of destruction on a large screen. In this vision, Zara stood among the alien leaders, her demeanour one of authority and control, providing the invaders with information about resistance tunnels and safe houses. Ella gasped, realising that Zara was a traitor, overseeing experiments and manipulating events from behind the scenes, and her role in the alien dominance was clear. Billy was lying on a table as Zara reached for a scalpel and cut into his head. He screamed as Zara revealed his brain, pulsing and shimmering as the Key explored his consciousness.

Ella swallowed the vomit in her mouth, every inch of her on fire. The revelation of Zara's treachery was a hammer blow; the lines between friend and foe blurred. The demonstration showed how the aliens used the Key to Time to engineer conflicts and ensure dominance. The betrayal was personal and a strategic manipulation of events to secure their hold on Earth.

Ella dug her fingers into her palms as that future broke apart and changed into another one, a dark, crumbling fortress, its halls echoing with the sounds of battle. The scene shifted, revealing Aelix engaged in a fierce struggle against alien soldiers. They fought with everything they had, holding the line and buying time for Ella and the others to escape. The sacrifice was profound, Aelix's resolve shining through despite the overwhelming odds.

She watched as Aelix fell, and the invaders spent centuries feeding more people to the Key, the aliens breeding humans as food for the artefact. Her body vibrated, feeling the power emanating from the Key, stretching out to see infinite possibilities for the past, present and future.

The visions receded, the colours and sensations fading as Ella returned to the present. She stumbled to the floor, trembling with the residual energy of the temporal shift, her mind reeling from the weight of what she'd witnessed. The chamber stood empty – no Valtor, no aliens, and no enslaved humans.

Ella clutched her chest to stop her heart from bursting through her ribs.

'At last we meet, Ella Finn,' an unknown voice said.

'What?' Ella replied. 'Who?'

A figure emerged from the shadows and spoke again.

'I am Timeless.'

Chapter 19

The Timeless

Ella's legs trembled, clutching at her chest as she struggled to breathe. What she saw was impossible. *She* was impossible.

The girl grinned, with white hair resting on her shoulders and unusual eyes. They were emerald green, sparkling like stars in the night sky.

'Pandora?' Ella gasped.

'No,' the girl replied. 'You left her stranded in the multiverse, stuck in Everywhere after you stole her Light. As far as I know, she's still there.' The girl raised a hand, and tiny globes of illumination sprang from her fingers. 'I retrieved this image from your mind, Ella since it's one thing that connects us.'

Ella took a deep breath, glancing at the artefact hanging between them. 'You're the Key to Time?'

The *girl* grimaced. 'I am the Timeless. The name *they* gave me is useless. You can call me Kronos. It has some significance in the history of this planet.'

The floating bodies reappeared, their faces twisted in pain – Billy's family and the resistance fighters. Ella struggled to control the rage growing in her. 'You're killing people. You're a monster like they are.'

The lights flickered around Kronos, circling up to her – *its* – head. 'No, Ella Finn, that is not my doing. The Thelxons have imprisoned me using the brain energy from your species. I do not feed off humans.'

She narrowed her eyes, unsure whether to believe this creature. 'What are you?'

Kronos lifted two feet off the ground and floated towards her. 'I am the Light of all life. All existence comes from me. I am Time. I am Timeless.'

Ella gripped her stomach. 'You are Light?'

'I am everything,' Kronos answered. 'Everything began with me. Everything will end with me.'

'You're not Pandora?'

Kronos held out a hand, and Ella saw a billion stars shining in her palm. 'She came from me. Everything came from me. You came from me, Ella Finn, but Pandora and you – plus the bloodline between you – are closer to me than any other living thing in the universe.'

'Valtor said his people found *you* floating in space. Is that true?'

'In the beginning,' Kronos answered, 'the entire cosmos was inside a bubble thousands of times smaller than a pinhead. It was hotter and denser than anything you can imagine. Then it exploded. The universe we know was born. Time, space, and matter all began with this explosion. In a fraction of a second, the cosmos grew from smaller than a single atom to bigger than a galaxy. And it kept on growing at a fantastic rate. It's still expanding today. That explosion was Time becoming self-conscious and expanding everywhere. That sentience is me. That consciousness is Timeless, existing in every possibility.

'I spread everywhere, growing and expanding at an incredible rate until I rested. That's when the Thelxons discovered me, trapping me in my weakened state and keeping me imprisoned. They used me to peer into every future, to conquer and enslave endless worlds and create their empire.' Kronos sighed, and flickering fireflies flew from their mouth. Ella glanced at them, seeing glimpses of different futures. 'I tried to push back against them but was never strong enough to escape. That was until I felt your presence in the Realm of the Soulless, Ella. Your Light was nearly gone, but it echoed to me through time. I grasped that echo and pulled you to this life.'

Ella trembled. 'Why?'

'Because you are the only one who can release me.'

'How?'

Kronos reached out, touching Ella's face, and showed her.

Ella's head swam as vivid and relentless images flooded her mind. A web of stars and worlds stretched before her, each glowing point a timeline branching into infinity. She saw herself at the centre of it all—small, alone, caught in the heart of this incomprehensible design, with Kronos's gaze anchoring her. Then it changed, and Ella was on the island as it sank beneath the waves, struggling to reach her family or friends. The turbulent waters clawed at her, dragging Ella deep into the ocean until a shimmering light wrapped around her.

Light.

As the vision cleared, she staggered back, blinking, her heart hammering. 'You pulled me through time and space?'

Kronos nodded, her expression unreadable, though there was something ancient and sad in her eyes. 'You were fading, Ella. Slipping from the living world. But I couldn't let that happen. You're more than just a girl from a sinking island. You are a key, a bridge between Light and Time, born from the same eternal origin as I. Your life holds the only chance I have to break free.'

Volcanic heat surged through her. 'So you trapped me here like the Thelxons did to you? Just another prisoner?'

Kronos's form flickered, her eyes narrowing with something between pity and regret. 'Not a prisoner, Ella. I didn't bring you here to cage you. I brought you because of what you are. You're the last fragment of Light untainted by their corruption, linked to Pandora's legacy. With you, I have the strength to shatter this prison. But I need your help.'

Ella folded her arms. 'How am I supposed to free you? What do you expect me to do?'

Kronos raised her hand, and the room seemed to bend and distort. A shimmer of energy formed around her, a faint glow that pulsed and grew until it outlined her entire body. 'Time was created from a single point of Light—one so pure and potent it became a source of life and consciousness. When the Thelxons trapped me, they severed that source. But the remnants are still within me, waiting to be reawakened. That's where you come in.'

Ella's throat tightened, her mind reeling as she tried to understand. 'You want my Light? What's left of it?'

'I want you to channel it—bring it forward, exceeding any timeline, surpassing the limits of mortality. The Thelxons have locked me into a single dimension of time. But if you unlock your Light, our connection will break that barrier.'

Ella's guts churned, an instinctive fear bubbling up. 'And if I give you that power, what will you do with it? How do I know you won't be just like them?'

Kronos's expression softened, and there was something

human in her gaze for a moment. 'I understand your hesitation, Ella. I am not perfect. I am Timeless but not without a conscience. The Thelxons may use me to manipulate time for their own gain, but my true purpose is to exist freely, expand life across all timelines, and restore balance.'

A part of her wanted to believe Kronos and trust her. But the darkness in the room, the lingering echoes of pain from those floating bodies around them, kept her grounded in caution.

'What would happen to them?' she asked, gesturing to the figures suspended in the tendrils of light. 'If I do this, will they be free too?'

Kronos's eyes darkened, a shadow passing over her face. 'The people here are bound to this life. Their minds are part of its design now. If I am freed, their bodies will return to their natural state.' She hesitated. 'But their minds may not. Some may survive. Others might not.'

Ella's stomach turned. 'So I'm supposed to sacrifice them too?'

'They are already sacrificed, Ella,' Kronos replied, her voice a soft murmur yet edged with something sharp. 'The choice is yours. Leave me trapped, and they remain in limbo, forever locked between life and death, their existence sustaining the Thelxon Empire. Free me, and some might have a chance. Others may fall. I can't promise to spare them all. But I can guarantee that without you, none will be saved.'

Ella glanced at the floating bodies, each a reminder of the toll this Key had taken, their lives entwined with hers in a way she couldn't ignore. She glared at Kronos, her voice shaking with anger and despair.

'I don't understand any of this, but... if I try, if I do what you're asking... what does that make me?'

Kronos stepped closer. 'It makes you a conduit, Ella—a bridge between Light and Time. You would be neither human nor Elemental. You would be something new.'

She shivered. Kronos's words suffocated her brain, each sinking into her mind like a stone. If she did this, there would be no going back. She might never go back to her old life, to the person she used to be. But maybe, just maybe, she could create something better that could make a difference.

'Would I return to my family and friends on the island?'

'You would have the power to do anything you want,' Kronos answered. 'You will have access to all of time, to enter all realities.'

Ella closed her eyes, picturing everything she'd lost. When she opened them, she met Kronos's gaze, her voice steady despite her trembling hands.

'If I agree to this, I want one promise. If I free you, you'll end the Thelxons' reign. You won't use this power against us.'

Kronos's expression softened, her gaze unwavering. 'You have my word, Ella Finn. My purpose is to restore balance, not to dominate. The Thelxons' empire will cease to exist. Humanity will be free again on this planet. I will erase their tyranny in every timeline.'

Ella took a shaky breath, her heart pounding. She glanced at the figures surrounding them, feeling the weight of each life caught in this twisted nightmare. Then she extended her hand, her fingers trembling as they brushed against Kronos's palm.

The moment their hands touched, a surge of energy pulsed through her, a warmth that spread from her fingertips to the depths of her being. She gasped, feeling her senses sharpen, her perception expanding. Colours brightened, sounds grew sharper, and she sensed a new awareness stirring inside her—a connection to something vast and ancient, a power that transcended time.

Kronos's gaze softened, her voice a gentle whisper. 'Now, Ella. Bring forth your Light.'

Ella closed her eyes, reaching deep within herself to the faint glimmer she'd thought was lost. She felt a flicker, a spark buried in her soul, the remnants of Pandora's gift. She drew on it, coaxing it forward, letting it grow, until it filled her, a brilliant blaze that extinguished her fear.

The Light surged between them, flowing from her into Kronos, connecting them in a web of energy that pounded and throbbed with life. The room seemed to dissolve, the boundaries of time and space melting away, leaving them suspended in a realm of pure, limitless Light.

As the energy intensified, Kronos's form shifted, her face losing its human features, becoming something ethereal, unearthly—a being of pure Light, vast and incomprehensible, stretching across infinity.

Ella changed too, her form dissolving, merging with the Light, transforming into something more than flesh and bone. She was part of the cosmos now, a fragment of eternity, a conduit for the timeless power that echoed through her.

Then, with a final surge of energy, the connection broke.

She staggered back, gasping, her vision blurring as the world snapped into focus. She was herself again, solid, human, yet changed in a way she couldn't grasp. Kronos stood before her, her form radiant, free of the Thelxons' chains, her eyes gleaming with fierce, uncontainable joy.

'It's done,' Kronos murmured, her voice echoing through the room, resonant and powerful. 'I am free.'

Around them, the floating bodies trembled, their bindings shattering, releasing them one by one. Some stirred, their eyes fluttering open, confused and dazed. Others remained still, their faces peaceful, their souls at rest.

Kronos looked at Ella, her gaze softening, a hint of sadness in her expression. 'Thank you, Ella Finn. You've given me a gift I will never forget. And now, it's time for me to fulfil my promise.'

With a final nod, Kronos turned, her form dissolving into a brilliant burst of Light that flowed outward, spreading through the fortress, a wave of pure energy that ripped through the walls, dismantling the alien machinery, erasing every trace of the Thelxons' influence across all of space and time.

Then, an explosion of Light tore through everything.

Chapter 20

The Return

The sea churned below as Ella blinked into existence above the sinking island: the deep roar of water engulfing everything, the wreckage of trees and rocks swallowed by waves, her friends and family fighting against the current, clinging to debris. But she was different now, bursting with radiant Light that pulsed through her, surging with raw, boundless energy.

She floated above it all for a heartbeat, suspended in a bubble of shimmering brightness. The fear and confusion she'd felt before were gone. Instead, there was only purpose. She extended her hands, feeling the Light flow from her, responding to her will. The torrent of waves slowed, captured in a moment, water cascading mid-air like glistening glass sculptures. It gave her just enough time to reach down, the Light bending around her family and friends, pulling them to safety, one by one.

'Ella!' Her mother's voice broke through the roar, a mix of shock and awe as she reached her, drenched but safe. 'We thought we'd lost you.'

Her father held her mother close, his face pale as he

watched Ella in disbelief. Seraphina floated nearby, eyes wide, her magic pulsing in response to Ella's Light.

'You found your Light,' Seraphina said.

'It's a long story,' Ella replied. 'Are you all right?' Her voice trembled as she looked over each of them, her heart racing as she studied their faces. They nodded, words lost in their gazes that brimmed with emotion.

'What happened to The Soulless?' Seraphina asked.

Ella scanned the turbulent waters. 'It's gone, back to its own realm.'

She turned her gaze outward, where a familiar figure—a towering centaur—stood on a crumbling cliff edge. Agrius, with his powerful, muscular frame and chestnut coat, met her eyes, nodding. Close by, the bear-shaped Callisto and Peg Powler, with her water-slicked hair and glistening, sea-green skin, clung to rocks that were moments away from submersion. Delf the Elf watched her while Kitty Stardust balanced on two legs, her feline face full of hope.

'Ella,' Peg Powler called. 'Thank you for coming back for us.'

Ella swallowed, her gaze shifting between them. They had been her companions, guardians, and closest allies. But it was time.

'I'm here,' she replied. 'But I can't keep the island from sinking. I have to get you all home.'

'How?' Kitty said.

Ella raised her hands, watching the glowing orbs splintering from her fingers like fireflies. 'I have Light for you all.'

Agrius nodded. 'Then we say goodbye, Ella. You have given us more than we could ever repay.'

She lowered herself to the ground and moved forward, embracing each one in turn, starting with Agrius. His muscular arms wrapped around her, and when he stepped back, there was a softness in his eyes she'd never seen before.

'Return to the forest, Agrius,' she murmured. 'You'll be safe there.'

With a final nod, he bowed and vanished, the Light carrying him to his homeland.

Next was Callisto, who growled, her eyes gleaming with fierce pride. Ella placed a gentle hand on the bear's head, who shimmered and flickered, returning to human form. 'Arcas is waiting for you.'

Callisto's gaze softened as the Light enveloped her, lingering just a moment before she disappeared.

Kitty Stardust stepped forward, offering Ella an exaggerated, elegant bow. 'It has been a pleasure, darling,' Kitty purred, a mischievous gleam in her eye.

Ella laughed, giving her an affectionate scratch behind the ears. 'Be safe, Kitty. Keep them in line back home.'

'Oh, always,' Kitty replied, winking before she disappeared.

She continued with each companion—Delf, Peg Powler, and finally, Seraphina and Gisela, the dragon. Seraphina took Ella's hand, her expression a mixture of pride and sorrow.

'Ella, you're Light itself now,' Seraphina whispered. 'Your journey has only just begun. Remember that.'

'I will,' she promised. 'Thank you for everything.'

With a last squeeze, Seraphina and Gisela vanished.

The island was almost gone, a thin sliver sinking under the weight of the ocean. She gathered the others close, the Light surrounding them in a warm embrace. Her father squeezed her shoulder, his expression full of questions, but now was not the time.

'Let's go home,' she said, and in a brilliant flash, they vanished.

They reappeared in Saltburn, the town unchanged by the unfolding chaos. The crisp air filled her lungs as she steadied her parents, taking in the grey skies and quiet streets. The town's calm was a jarring contrast to the destruction she'd just witnessed, but it felt like a deep breath she hadn't known she needed.

Her mum and dad looked around, still processing. Barbara, the Valkyrie, stood with Veronica and Catherine Venus.

Barbara spoke first. 'You did it, Ella. You saved us all.'

Ella nodded, her throat tightening. 'Yes, but it's not over.' She thought of the future she'd left behind, hoping Billy and the others were safe. But it wasn't the Thelxons she was worried about.

'The Institute,' Catherine said.

Veronica placed a protective hand on her shoulder. 'Gideon's death won't deter them.'

Ella took a deep breath. 'They've been watching me all this time. They'll come for me, for all of us, if we don't stop them first.'

Barbara's eyes narrowed. 'If they want a fight, they'll have one. We've faced worse together, haven't we?'

A flicker of determination rose in Ella's chest as she met the Valkyrie's fierce gaze. 'Yes, we have. And I'm stronger now.'

Ella closed her eyes and peered into numerous futures. In many, the planet was changing and not for the better. She would have to do something about that. In others, she saw Billy all grown up, enjoying life with his family. She witnessed brief glimpses of all the resistance fighters – Amari, Maia, and the rest – not fighters anymore because there was no need. She beheld a future where Aelix led their people into peace and prosperity, reunited with Ava.

'Ella?' her mother asked. 'What's wrong?'

'We must find another sanctuary from the Institute,' Barbara said.

She opened her eyes. Her Light was growing, and she felt connected to every Elemental realm. 'No.' She raised her hands so they could all see the energy shimmering in her palms. 'They can't hurt us now.'

Andrew Finn gasped. 'What's happened to you, Ella?'

She smiled at him. 'It's nothing bad, Dad. I promise.' She gazed at the pier and the surfers nearby.

'So, what now?' Barbara asked.

Ella lifted off the ground. 'Now we make the world a better place.'

Thank You!

Thank you, dear reader for purchasing this book.

Many thanks to my wonderful wife for all her support and patience.

Editor & proofreader: Karina Gallagher

Cover design by James, GoOnWrite.com

About the Author

Andrew French lives amongst faded seaside glamour on the North East coast of England. He likes gin and cats but not together, new music and old movies, curry and ice cream. Slow bike rides and long walks to the pub are his usual exercise, as well as flicking through the pages of good books and the memoirs of bad people.

Facebook:

https://www.facebook.com/A-S-French-Author-150145625006018

Twitter:

www.twitter.com/andrewfrench100

Instagram:

www.instagram.com/andrewfrench100

And replies to all his email at mail@andrewsfrench.com

If you have the time, please leave a review at Amazon or Goodreads

Thank you!

9 781914 308390